ME AND YOU

Also by Niccolò Ammaniti

I'm Not Scared
I'll Steal You Away
As God Commands

ME AND YOU

by Niccolò Ammaniti

Translated by Kylee Doust

BLACK CAT
New York
a paperback original imprint of Grove/Atlantic, Inc.

First published in Italy in 2010 as Io e Te
by Giulio Einaudi editore, Torino.
Translation first published in English in Great Britain in 2012
by Canongate Books Ltd. Edinburgh

Printed in the United States of America

ISBN-13: 978-0-8021-7090-3

Black Cat
a paperback original imprint of Grove/Atlantic, Inc.
841 Broadway
New York, NY 10003
Distributed by Publishers Group West
www.groveatlantic.com

12 13 14 15   10 9 8 7 6 5 4 3 2 1

And this one's for my mother and father

In a real dark night of the soul, it is always
three o'clock in the morning.
F. Scott Fitzgerald, 'The Crack-Up'

But can you save me?
Come on and save me
If you could save me
From the ranks of the freaks
Who suspect they could never love anyone.
Aimee Mann, 'Save Me'

Batesian mimicry occurs when a harmless animal species takes advantage of its similarity to a toxic or poisonous species that inhabits the same territory, imitating its colouring and behaviour. In this way, the imitating species is associated in the predators' minds with the dangerous one, increasing its chances of survival.

Cividale del Friuli

12 January 2010

'Coffee?'

A waitress is studying me over the top of her glasses. She's holding a silver coffee pot.

I put out my cup. 'Thank you.'

She fills it up to the brim. 'Are you here for the fair?'

I shake my head. 'What fair?'

'The horse fair.' She looks at me. She's waiting for me to tell her why I happen to be in Cividale del Friuli. In the end she pulls out a notebook. 'What's your room number?'

I show her the key. 'One hundred and nineteen.'

She writes down the number. 'If you'd like any more coffee you can serve yourself from the buffet.'

'Thanks.'

'My pleasure.'

As soon as she moves away I pull a piece of paper folded into four out of my wallet. I flatten it on the table.

My sister Olivia wrote it ten years ago, the twenty-fourth of February 2000.

I was fourteen years old and she was twenty-three.

Rome

Ten years earlier

1

On the evening of the eighteenth of February 2000 I went to bed early and dropped off straight away, but during the night I woke up and wasn't able to get back to sleep.

At ten minutes past six, with the feather quilt pulled up underneath my chin, I was breathing with my mouth open.

The house was quiet. The only sounds I could hear were the rain tapping against the window, my mother walking backwards and forwards between the bedroom and the bathroom upstairs, and the air going in and out of my throat. Soon she would come and wake me up to take me to the meeting with the others. I turned on the cricket-shaped lamp that sat on the bedside table.

The green light painted the slice of the room where my backpack sat, swollen with clothes, beside the waterproof jacket and the bag with my ski boots and skis.

Between my thirteenth and fourteenth birthdays I'd had a growth spurt, as if they'd put fertiliser on me, and I was taller than my peers. My mother said that two carthorses had stretched me. I spent a lot of time in front of the mirror studying my white skin stained with freckles, the hairs on my legs. On the top of my head grew a hazel bush that had ears sticking out of it. The shape of my face had been remodelled by puberty, and a substantial nose separated two green eyes.

I got up and I slid my hand into the pocket of the backpack.

'The pocket knife's there. So is the torch. I've got everything,' I whispered.

My mother's footsteps moved down the hallway. She must be wearing the blue high heels, I thought.

I dived back into bed, turned off the light and pretended to be asleep.

'Lorenzo, wake up. It's late.'

I lifted my head off the pillow and rubbed my eyes.

My mother pulled up the shutters. 'It's a foul day . . . Let's hope the weather's better in Cortina.'

The gloomy light of the dawn reflected her thin silhouette. She was wearing the grey skirt and jacket that she used when she did important stuff. Her round-necked cardigan. Her pearls. And her blue high heels.

'Good morning,' I yawned, as if I'd just woken up.

She sat down on the edge of the bed. 'Did you sleep well, darling?'

'Yes.'

'I'm going to make you breakfast . . . You go have a shower in the meantime.'

'What about Nihal?'

She combed my hair with her fingers. 'He's still asleep. Did he give you your ironed T-shirts?'

I nodded.

'Get up, come on.'

I wanted to, but a weight on my chest was suffocating me.

'What's the matter?'

I took her hand. 'Do you love me?'

She smiled. 'Of course I love you.' She stood up, looked at her reflection in the mirror beside the door and smoothed out her skirt.

'Get up, come on. On a day like today do I have to beg you to get out of bed?'

'Kiss.'

She bent over me. 'Look, you're not joining the army, you're going skiing for a week.'

I hugged her and slid my head under her blonde hair, which hung over her face, and I put my nose against her neck.

She had a nice smell. It made me think of Morocco. Of its narrow alleyways full of stalls with coloured powders. But I had never been to Morocco.

'What perfume is that?'

'It's sandalwood soap. The usual.'

'Can you lend it to me?'

She raised an eyebrow. 'Why?'

'So I can wash myself with it and carry you with me.'

She pulled the covers off me. 'That would be a first, you washing yourself. Come on, don't be silly, you won't have time to think about me.'

Through the car window I studied the wall of the zoo covered in wet election posters. Higher up, inside the aviary where they kept the birds of prey, a vulture was sitting on a dry branch. It looked like an old woman dressed in mourning, asleep in the rain.

The heating inside the car made it hard to breathe and the biscuits I'd had for breakfast were stuck at the back of my throat.

The rain was easing up. A couple – he was fat, she was skinny – were doing exercises on the leaf-covered steps of the Modern Art Museum.

I looked at my mother.

'What is it?' she said, without taking her eyes off the road.

I puffed up my chest, trying to imitate my father's low voice: 'Arianna, you should wash this car. It's a pigsty on wheels.'

She didn't laugh. 'Did you say goodbye to your father?'

'Yes.'

'What did he say?'

'Not to be silly and not to ski like a maniac.' I paused. 'And not to call you every five minutes.'

'Is that what he said?'

'Yes.'

She changed gear and turned down Flaminia. The city was beginning to fill up with cars.

'Call me whenever you want. Have you got everything? Your music? Your mobile?'

'Yes.'

13

The grey sky hung heavily above the roofs and between the antennas.

'Did you pack the bag with the medicines? Did you put the thermometer in there?'

'Yes.'

A guy on a Vespa laughed into the mobile stuck under his helmet.

'Money?'

'Yes.'

We crossed the bridge over the Tiber.

'We checked the rest together yesterday evening. You've got everything.'

'Yes, I've got everything.'

We were waiting at the stoplight. A woman in a Fiat 500 was staring in front of her. An old man was dragging two Labradors along the footpath. A seagull was crouching on the skeleton of a tree covered in plastic bags that stuck out of the mud-coloured water.

If God had come and asked me if I wanted to be that seagull, I would have answered yes.

I undid my seat belt. 'Drop me off here.'

She looked at me as if she hadn't understood. 'What do you mean, here?'

'I mean, here.'

The light turned green.

'Pull over, please.'

But she kept on driving. Luckily there was a rubbish truck that slowed us down.

'Mum! Pull over.'

'Put your seatbelt back on.'

'Please stop.'

'But why?'

'I want to get there on my own.'

'I don't understand . . .'

I raised my voice. 'Stop, please.'

My mother pulled over, turned off the engine and pulled her hair back with her hand. 'What's going on? Lorenzo, please, let's not start . . . You know I'm no good at this time of the morning.'

'It's just that . . .' I squeezed my hands into a fist. 'Everyone else is going there on their own. I can't turn up with you. I'll look like a loser.'

'What are you saying?' She rubbed her eyes. 'I'm supposed to just leave you here?'

'Yes.'

'And I don't even thank Alessia's parents?'

I shrugged. 'There's no need. I'll thank them for you.'

'Not on your life.' And she turned the key in the ignition.

I flung myself on her. 'No . . . No . . . Please.'

She pushed me back. 'Please, what?'

'Let me go by myself. I can't turn up with my mummy. They'll make fun of me.'

'That's just silly . . . I want to make sure that everything is all right, if I have to do anything. It's the least I can do. I'm not rude like you.'

'I'm not rude. I'm just like all the others.'

She flicked the indicator on. 'No. No way.'

I hadn't counted on my mother caring this much about taking me there.

The anger was starting to build. I started banging my fists on my legs.

'What are you doing now?'

'Nothing.' I squeezed the door handle until my knuckles were white. I could rip off the rear-view mirror and smash the car window.

'Why do you have to act like a child?'

'You're the one who treats me like a . . . dickhead.'

She stared daggers at me. 'Don't swear. You know I can't stand it. And there's no need for you to make such a scene.'

I punched the dashboard. 'Mum, I want to go there on my own, for Christ's sake.' The anger was pushing against my throat. 'All right. I won't go. Are you happy?'

'Look, I am really getting cross, Lorenzo.'

I had one last card to play. 'Everybody else said they were going there on their own. I'm the only one who always turns up with his mummy. That's why I have these issues . . .'

'Now don't make me out to be the one who causes your problems.'

'Dad said I have to be independent. That I have to have my own life. That I have to break away from you.'

My mother closed her eyes and pressed her thin lips together as if she were trying to stop herself from talking. She turned around and stared at the cars driving by.

'This is the first time they've asked me along . . . what will they think of me?' I added.

She looked around as if she was hoping someone would tell her what to do.

I squeezed her hand. 'Mum, don't worry . . .'

She shook her head. 'No, I will worry.'

★   ★   ★

17

With my arm round the skis, the bag with the ski boots in my hand and the backpack on my shoulders I watched my mother do a U-turn. I waved and waited until the BMW had disappeared over the bridge.

I headed up Viale Mazzini. I went past the RAI building. About a metre before reaching via Col di Lana I slowed down. My heart beat faster. I had a bitter taste in my mouth like I'd been licking copper wire. All the stuff I was carrying made me clumsy. I felt like I was in a sauna inside my goose down jacket.

When I came to the intersection, I poked my head round the corner. At the end of the street, parked in front of a modern-style church, was a big Mercedes SUV. I could see Alessia Roncato, her mother, the Sumerian and Oscar Tommasi stuffing their luggage into the car boot. A Volvo with a pair of skis on the roof rack pulled up next to the SUV and Richard Dobosz got out and ran over to the others. Soon Dobosz's father also got out.

I drew back behind the wall. I put the skis down, unzipped my jacket and took another look around the corner.

Now Alessia's mother and Dobosz's father were

tying the skis to the roof rack. The Sumerian was hopping from side to side pretending to take a shot at Dobosz. Alessia and Oscar Tommasi were talking on their mobiles.

It took them ages to get ready. Alessia's mother kept getting angry with her daughter for not lending a hand; the Sumerian climbed up onto the car roof to check the skis.

And eventually they left.

I felt like an idiot as I rode the tram, with my skis and ski boots, squashed in between office clerks in ties and suits, mums and kids heading off to school. If I closed my eyes it felt like I was on the cable car. With Alessia, Oscar Tommasi, Dobosz and the Sumerian. I could smell the lip balm, the suntan lotion. We would have got off the cable car, pushing each other and laughing, talking loudly regardless of the people around us, like all those people my mother and father call yobs. I would have said funny things and have made them all laugh while they put their skis on. I would have done impressions of people, cracked jokes. But I was never able to say funny things in public. You have to be very confident to make jokes in public.

19

'Life is sad without a sense of humour,' I said.

'Amen,' answered a lady standing next to me.

My father had said this thing about a sense of humour after my cousin Vittorio had thrown a cowpat at me during a walk in the country. I was so angry I grabbed a huge rock and threw it at a tree, while that retard rolled on the ground with laughter. Even my father and mother had laughed.

I loaded the skis on to my shoulders and got off the tram.

I looked at my watch. Seven fifty.

Too early to go back home. I was sure to run into Dad as he left for work.

I headed towards Villa Borghese, to the valley near the zoo where dogs are allowed to run off the lead. I sat down on a bench, pulled a bottle of Coke out of my backpack and took a sip.

My mobile began ringing in my pocket.

I waited a moment before answering.

'Mum . . .'

'Everything all right?'

'Yes.'

'Are you on your way?'

'Yes.'

'Is there much traffic?'

A Dalmatian careered past me. 'A bit . . .'

'Can you put Alessia's mum on?'

I lowered my voice. 'She can't talk right now. She's driving.'

'Well, I'll speak to her this evening then, so I can thank her.'

The Dalmatian had begun barking at its owner because it wanted her to throw it a stick.

I put my hand over the phone and ran towards the street.

'All right.'

'Bye.'

'All right, Mum, bye . . . Hey, where are you? What are you doing?'

'Nothing. I'm in bed. I wanted to sleep a little more.'

'When are you going out?'

'I'll go and see your grandma later.'

'And Dad?'

'He's just left.'

'Ah . . . okay then.'

'Bye.'

Perfect.

★   ★   ★

21

There he was, the Silver Monkey, sweeping up the leaves. That's what I called Franchino, our building's doorman. He looked exactly like a kind of monkey that lives in the Congo. He had a round head covered with a strip of silver hair. This band began at the nape of his neck and curled up over his ears and down his jawline until it joined up on his chin. A single dark eyebrow crossed his forehead. Even the way he walked was strange. He moved forward hunched over, with his long arms swaying, the palms of his hands facing forwards and his head bobbing.

He was from Soverato, in Calabria, where his family lived. But he had worked in our building since forever. I thought he was nice. My mother and my father said that he was over-familiar with them.

Now the problem was how to get into the building without him seeing me.

The Silver Monkey moved very slowly and it took him a lifetime to sweep the courtyard. Hiding behind a truck parked on the other side of the street I pulled out my mobile and dialled his home number. The phone in his basement flat began ringing. It took the Silver Monkey ages to hear it.

At last he dumped the broom and loped towards the entrance. I watched him disappear down the stairs.

I grabbed the skis and boots and crossed the street. I just missed being hit by a Ka, which began honking at me. Behind it, other drivers had slammed on their brakes and were yelling insults.

Gritting my teeth, as the skis kept slipping and the backpack cut into my shoulders, I turned off my mobile and walked through the gates. I passed by the moss-covered fountain where the goldfish live and the English-style lawn with the marble benches you weren't allowed to sit on. My mother's car was parked next to the shelter near the main door, under the palm tree she had saved from the red palm weevil.

Praying that I wouldn't run into anyone on their way out of the building I slipped into the foyer, ran along the red carpet past the lift and dived down the stairs which led to the cellars.

When I made it downstairs I was out of breath. Patting my way along the wall I found the light switch. Two long, faded striplights came on, illuminating a narrow, windowless corridor. Along one side ran pipes, along the other, closed doors. Standing in front of the third door, I stuck my hand in my pocket, pulled out a long key and turned it in the lock.

The door opened onto a large, rectangular room. Up high, two small windows veiled with dust let in a sliver of light which fell on furniture covered with sheets, on boxes full of books, saucepans and clothes, on termite-ridden window frames, on tables and wooden doors, on lime-crusted sinks and stacks of upholstered chairs. Stuff was piled up everywhere I looked. A flowery blue settee. A heap of mildewed mattresses. A collection of moth-eaten *Reader's Digest*s. Old records. Crooked lampshades. A cast iron bedhead. Rugs rolled up in newspapers. A big ceramic bulldog with a broken paw.

A Fifties household amassed in a cellar.

But over on one side was a mattress with blankets and a pillow. Neatly set out on top of a coffee table were ten tins of corned beef, twenty of tuna, three bags of sliced bread, six jars of vegetables in oil, twelve bottles each of Ferrarelle sparkling water, fruit juice and Coke, a jar of Nutella, two tubes of mayonnaise, biscuits, snacks and two bars of milk chocolate. A small television sat on a chest, along with my PlayStation, three Stephen King novels and a couple of Marvel comics.

I locked the door.

This would be my ski week.

2

I started talking when I was three years old. Small talk has never been one of my strengths. If someone I didn't know said something to me I would answer yes, no, I don't know. And if they insisted, I would answer with whatever they wanted to hear me say.

Once you've thought something, what need is there to say it aloud?

'Lorenzo, you're like a cactus: you grow without bothering anyone, you just need a drop of water and a bit of light,' an old nanny from Caserta used to say to me.

My parents used to bring over au pairs for me to play with. But I preferred playing on my own. I would close the door and imagine that my room was a cube that floated through space.

My problems started at primary school.

I have very few memories of that period. I remember my teachers' names, the hydrangeas in the schoolyard, the metal containers full of steaming hot maccheroni in the canteen. And the others.

The others were anyone who wasn't my mum, my father and Grandma Laura.

If the others didn't leave me alone, if they pushed me too far, the blood would rise up through my legs, flood my stomach and spread out to the tips of my hands, and then I would clench my fists and lash out.

When I pushed Giampolo Tinari off the wall and he fell on his head on the cement and had to get stitches in his forehead, they called home.

In the staff room, my teacher told my mother: 'He looks like he's at the station waiting for the train to take him home. He doesn't annoy anyone, but if any of his classmates tease him he starts shouting, turns red and starts throwing whatever he can get his hands on.' The teacher had studied the floor, embarrassed. 'Sometimes he is frightening. I don't know . . . I would recommend you . . .'

My mother took me to see Professor Masburger. 'You'll see. He helps a lot of kids.'

'But how long do I have to go for?'

'Three quarters of an hour. Twice a week. What do you say?'

'Yeah, that's not too much,' I told her.

If my mother thought I'd end up being like the others that was fine with me. Everyone had to think that I was normal, Mum included.

Nihal would take me. A fat secretary wearing a caramel perfume would lead me into a mouldy-smelling room with a low ceiling. The window faced a grey wall. On the hazelnut-coloured walls hung old black and white photos of Rome.

'But does everyone who has problems lie there?' I asked Professor Masburger, as he pointed towards a faded brocade couch.

'Of course. Everyone. This way you can talk more freely.'

Perfect. I would pretend to be a normal kid with problems. It wouldn't take much to trick him. I knew exactly how the others reasoned, what they liked and what they wished for. And if what I knew wasn't enough, that couch I was lying on would transfer to me, like a warm body transfers heat to a cold body, the thoughts of the kids that had lain there before me.

And so I told him all about a different Lorenzo.

A Lorenzo who was embarrassed to talk to the others but who wanted to be like them. I liked pretending that I loved the others.

A few weeks after I began the therapy I heard my parents whispering in the living room. I went into the study. I took a few volumes from the bookshelves and put my ear up against the wall.

'So what's wrong with him?' Father was saying.

'He said that he has a narcissistic personality disorder.'

'What does that mean?'

'He says that Lorenzo is unable to feel empathy for others. For him everything that's outside his circle of affections doesn't exist, has no effect on him. He believes he is special and only people as special as him can understand him.'

'You want to know what I think? That this Masburger is a dickhead. I have never seen any boy as affectionate as our son.'

'That's true, but only with us, Francesco. Lorenzo thinks that we're the special people and he considers everyone else to be inferior.'

'He's a snob? Is that what the professor is trying to tell us?'

'He said that he has an inflated sense of self-importance.'

My father burst into laughter. 'Thank goodness. Just think if he had a low sense of self-importance. That's enough, take him away from that worthless idiot before he fills up our son's brain with nonsense for good. Lorenzo is a normal child.'

'Lorenzo is a normal child,' I repeated to myself.

Little by little I worked out how I should act at school. I had to keep to myself, but not too much, otherwise I stuck out.

I was like a sardine in a school of sardines. I camouflaged myself like a stick insect on dry branches. And I learned to control my anger. I imagined that I had a tank in my stomach, and when it filled up I emptied it out through my feet and the anger ended up in the ground and penetrated into the world's guts and was burned up by the eternal flames.

Now nobody bothered me.

For middle school I was sent to St Joseph's, an English school filled with the children of diplomats, of foreign artists who had fallen in love with Italy, of managers from the US and of wealthy Italians who could afford the fees. Everyone was out of place there. They all spoke different languages and looked like they were just passing through. The girls kept to themselves and the guys played football on the big field opposite the school. I fitted in well.

But my parents weren't satisfied. I had to have friends.

Football was a stupid game, everyone running around after a ball, but that's what everyone else liked. If I learned to play, I was home free. I would have some friends.

I found the courage and put myself in goal, where nobody ever wanted to play. I realised that defending it from enemy attacks wasn't all that bad. There was this one guy, Angelo Stangoni, who was unstoppable whenever he got the ball. He would shoot like a lightning bolt to the goal and kick really hard. One day a defender knocked him down with a kick. Penalty. I lined myself up in the middle of the goal. He took a run up.

I am not a man, I said to myself, I am a nyuzzo, a hideous but incredibly agile animal produced in an Umbrian laboratory that has just one purpose in life: to defend the earth from a mortal meteorite.

Stangoni kicked hard, straight down the line, and I flew like only a nyuzzo can, stretching out my arms. And the ball was there in my hands. I saved it.

I remember how all my team-mates hugged me and it was nice because they thought I was one of them.

They put me on the team. Suddenly I had schoolmates who called me at home. My mother would answer and she was happy to be able to say: 'Lorenzo, it's for you.'

I used to say I was going over to my friend's house but really I went and hid out at Grandma Laura's. She lived on the top floor of an apartment building near ours, with Pericle, an old Basset Hound, and Olga, her Russian carer. We spent our afternoons playing canasta. She would drink Bloody Marys and I would have tomato juice with pepper and salt. We had made a pact: she wouldn't tell about my not going out with my friends and I wouldn't tell about her drinking Bloody Marys.

But middle school was soon over and my father called me into his study, sat me down in an armchair and said, 'Lorenzo, I think it's time you went to a public high school. You've had enough of these private schools for spoiled kids. So, what would you prefer, mathematics or history?'

I glanced quickly at all his heavy volumes on the ancient Egyptians and on the Babylonians, neatly lined up on his bookshelf. 'History.'

He gave me a satisfied pat on the shoulder. 'Excellent, old boy, we like the same things. You'll enjoy the Classics high school, you'll see.'

When I walked up to the entrance of the high school on my first day I almost fainted.

It was hell on earth. There were hundreds of kids. It felt like I was standing outside the gates of a rock concert. Some of them were way bigger than me. They even had beards. The girls had tits. They rode scooters, skateboards. Some were running. Some were laughing. Some were yelling. They were going in and out of the cafeteria. One guy climbed up a tree and hung a girl's backpack on a branch and she threw stones at him.

Anxiety took my breath away. I leaned up

against a wall covered in graffiti. Why did I have to go to school? Why did the world work like this? You are born, you go to school, you work and you die. Who had decided that that was the right way? Couldn't we live differently? Like primitive man? Like Grandma Laura, who when she was little had studied at home and had the teachers come to her. Why couldn't I do that too? Why didn't they just leave me alone? Why did I have to be just like the others? Couldn't I live by myself in a forest in Canada?

'I am not like them. I have an inflated sense of self-importance,' I whispered, as three colossal beasts walking arm in arm pushed me aside like I was a bowling pin. 'Piss off, shrimp.'

In a trance I felt my legs as stiff as tree trunks walk me into class. I sat in the second last row, near the window, and tried to make myself invisible. But I realised that the camouflage technique didn't work in this hostile planet. In this school the predators had evolved, were much more aggressive and they moved in herds. Any introversion, any unusual behaviour, was immediately noticed and punished.

They called me out. They picked on me for

the way I dressed, because I didn't talk. And then they stoned me with chalk dusters.

I begged my parents to let me change schools – one for misfits or deaf and dumb students would be perfect. I came up with every excuse in the book to stay home. I stopped studying. In class I spent my time counting the minutes left before I could get out of that jail.

One morning I was at home with a fake headache and I saw a documentary on television about insects that mimic other insects.

Somewhere, in the tropics, lives a fly that imitates wasps. He has four wings, just like the other flies, but he keeps them one on top of the other, so that they look like two. He has a black and yellow striped belly, antennae and bulbous eyes and even a fake stinger. He can't hurt you, he's a nice insect, but dressed up as a wasp, the birds, the lizards, even human beings fear him. He can mosey into a wasp nest, one of the most dangerous and well-protected places in the world, and go unrecognised.

I had been going about it the wrong way.

Here's what I had to do.

Imitate the dangerous ones.

I wore the same things the others wore. Adidas trainers, jeans with holes in them, a black hoodie. I messed up the parting in my hair and let it grow long. I even wanted to get my ear pierced but my mother forbade me. To make up for it, for Christmas, my parents gave me a scooter. The most popular one.

I walked like them, with my legs wide apart. I threw my backpack on the ground and kicked it around.

I mimicked them discreetly. There's a fine line between imitation and caricature.

During the lessons I sat at my desk pretending to listen – but in actual fact I was thinking about my own stuff, making up science-fiction stories. I even went to PE classes. I laughed at the others' jokes, I played stupid tricks on the girls. A couple of times I even answered back to the teachers. And I handed in a class test without answering a single question.

The fly had managed to trick them all, integrating perfectly with the waspian society. They thought I was one of them. That I was all right.

When I got home I told my parents that at school

everyone said I was cool, and I made up funny stories about things that had happened to me.

But the longer I put on this show, the more different I felt. The chasm that separated me from the others grew deeper. On my own I was happy, with the others I always had to pretend.

Sometimes this scared me. Would I have to imitate them for the rest of my life?

It was like the fly was inside me, telling me how things really were. It told me that it only took a second for friends to forget about you, that girls are mean and they make fun of you, that the world outside your house is filled with competition, violence and suffocation.

One night I had a nightmare and I woke up screaming. I discovered that my T-shirt and jeans were my skin and my trainers were my feet. My jacket was as hard as an exoskeleton, and under it wriggled one hundred insect feet.

Everything went along pretty smoothly until one morning I wished, for just a moment, that I wasn't a fly dressed up as a wasp, but that I was really a wasp.

During the break I would wander up and down

the crowded school corridors like I had something
to do, so that nobody got suspicious. Then just before
the bell rang I would sit back down at my desk and
eat my plain pizza with prosciutto, the same pizza
that everybody bought from the school janitor. In
the classroom the usual duster battle was taking
place. Two sides faced each other, throwing it back
and forth. If they happened to hit me, I would
retaliate, trying, if possible, not to hit anybody so
that I didn't set off any further retaliation.

Alessia Roncato was sitting behind me. She
and Oscar Tommasi were huddled together, talking
intensely and writing down a list of names on a
piece of paper.

What was on that list?

I shouldn't have cared, not at all, and yet my
stupid curiosity, which popped up occasionally
for no apparent reason, made me slide my chair
backwards to try and hear what they were saying.

'Do you reckon they'll let him come?' Oscar
Tommasi was saying.

'If my mum talks to them, yeah,' Alessia
Roncato answered.

'But can we all come?'

'Sure, it's really big . . .'

Somebody began to yell and I wasn't able to hear anything else. They were probably trying to work out who they should invite to some party.

On the way out I put my headphones on but I didn't turn on the music. Alessia Roncato and Oscar Tommasi were hanging out near the school wall with the Sumerian and Riccardo Dobosz. They were all excited. The Sumerian was pretending to ski. He kept bending down like he was doing a slalom. Dobosz jumped onto his back and pretended to strangle him. I had no way of knowing what Alessia was saying to Oscar Tommasi. But her eyes sparkled as she watched the Sumerian and Dobosz.

I moved over until I was just a couple of metres from the group, and in the end it was easy to work out what was going on.

Alessia had invited them all up to her house in Cortina for ski week.

Those four were different from the others. They kept to themselves and you could see that they were all best friends. It was like they had an invisible bubble around them that nobody else could get inside unless they wanted to let you in.

Alessia Roncato was the leader and she was the prettiest girl in the whole school. But she didn't show off, she didn't try to act like anyone else – she was herself, full stop.

Oscar Tommasi was skinny and walked like a girl. Whenever he said anything everyone burst into laughter.

Riccardo Dobosz was quiet and he always looked as serious as a samurai.

But the one I liked the most was the Sumerian. I don't know why they called him that. He had a motorcycle and he was good at all sports, and they said that he would become a champion rugby player. He was as big as a refrigerator, had hands like plasticine, a crew cut, a flat nose. I reckon if the Sumerian punched a Great Dane in the nose he could kill it on the spot. He was in fourth form, but he was never a bully with the younger kids. As far as he was concerned the kids from the lower classes were a bit like dust mites in his mattress. They were there but he couldn't see them.

They were the Fantastic Four and I was the Silver Surfer.

★   ★   ★

41

The Sumerian hopped on to his motorbike and pulled Alessia on, who hugged him like she was scared of losing him, and they took off, tyres screeching. One by one all the other students headed off home, and the street emptied. The CD shop and the white goods shop had pulled down their shutters for the lunch break.

I was the only one left.

I had to go home because if my mother didn't see me walk though the door in ten minutes' time she'd call me. I turned off my mobile. I stared at the graffiti until it went out of focus. Splashes of colour on the wall of a building.

If Alessia had invited me along too they would all have seen how good a skier I was. I would have shown them the secret slopes.

I had been going to Cortina since I was born. I knew all the slopes and loads of secret slopes too. My favourite began on Mount Cristallo and went all the way into the town centre. It took you through forests, there were some amazing jumps, and once I had seen two chamois deer behind a house. Then we could have gone to the cinema and got a hot chocolate at Lovat's.

I had so many things in common with them.

The fact that Alessia had a house in Cortina couldn't be just a coincidence. And that's when I realised. They too were flies pretending to be wasps. It was just that they were much better than I was. If I had gone with them to Cortina they would have realised that I was just like them.

When I got home my mother was teaching Nihal the recipe for osso buco. I sat down, opened and closed the cutlery drawer and said, 'Alessia Roncato invited me to go skiing with them in Cortina.'

My mother stared at me as if I'd told her I'd grown a tail. She looked around for a chair, took a deep breath and stuttered, 'Darling, I'm so happy.' And she hugged me really hard. 'It'll be lovely. Excuse me a second.' She got up, smiled at me and locked herself in the bathroom.

What was the matter with her?

I put my ear up against the door. She was crying, and every now and then she sniffed. Then I heard her turn on the tap and splash her face.

I was confused.

She began talking on her mobile. 'Francesco, I have to tell you something. Our son has been invited to go for ski week . . . Yes, in Cortina. See,

43

we don't have to worry . . . I'm so happy I burst into tears like an idiot. I locked myself in the bathroom so that he wouldn't notice . . .'

For a couple of days I tried to tell Mum that it was a lie, that I'd made it up just for fun, but each time I saw how happy and excited she was, I retreated in defeat, feeling like I had committed a murder.

The problem wasn't having to tell her that I had made everything up and that I hadn't been invited by anyone to go anywhere. It was humiliating, but I'd have been able to handle it. What I couldn't handle was the question that would have undoubtedly followed.

'But Lorenzo, why did you lie to me like that?'

And that was a question there was no answer to.

In my bedroom, at night, I tried to find one.

'Because . . .'

But it was as if I had a mental block.

'Because I'm a dickhead.' That was the only answer that came to mind. But I knew it wasn't enough, that underneath there was something I didn't want to face up to.

And so, in the end, I let myself go with the flow and I began to believe it. I even told the Silver Monkey about ski week. I was becoming more and more convincing. I embellished the story with details – we would stay in a refuge high up in the mountains and we would take a helicopter.

I threw a tantrum because I wanted my parents to buy me skis, ski boots and a new jacket. And as the days went by I began to believe that Alessia really had invited me along.

If I closed my eyes I could see her walking up to me. I was taking the chain off my scooter and she was looking at me with her blue eyes. She was running her fingers through her blonde fringe. She then put one Nike on top of the other and said to me, 'Listen, Lorenzo, I've organised a ski week. Do you want to come?'

I thought about it for a bit and then answered coolly, 'Okay, I'll come.'

Then, one day, while I was in my bedroom with my new ski boots on my feet, my gaze wandered to the mirror on the cupboard door and I saw the reflection of a young boy in underwear, as pasty white as a worm, with legs that looked like twigs, a total of four hairs on his body, a wimpy chest and those ridiculous red things on his feet, and after half a minute of studying him with my mouth half open I said, 'Where do you think you're going?'

And the young boy in the mirror answered me in a strangely adult-like voice: 'Nowhere.'

I threw myself on to the bed, ski boots and all, feeling like someone had dumped a ton of rubble on me, and I realised that I had no idea how to get out of the mess I had created and that if I tried again, even just once, to believe that Alessia had invited me to go with them, I would throw myself out the window, amen and ciao ciao and farewell and thanks for everything.

It was the simplest thing to do. My life sucked anyway.

'That's enough! I have to tell her that I can't go because Grandma Laura is in hospital and she's dying of cancer.' I put on a really serious voice and looking up at the ceiling I said, 'Mum, I've decided not to go skiing because Grandma's sick and what if she dies while I'm away?'

It was a great idea . . . I took off the ski boots and danced around the room like the floor was scorching hot. I jumped on the bed and from there onto the desk. I pirouetted around the computer, the books, the tank with the turtles, and began singing the national anthem: 'Fratelli d'Italia, l'Italia s'è desta.' A small leap and I was hanging from the bookshelves. 'Dell'elmo di Scipio . . .'

What was I doing?

'S'è cinta la te . . . sta.'

Was I trying to use Grandma's death to save myself?

Only a monster like me could even think of doing such a terrible thing.

'Shame on you!' I yelled and I threw myself onto the bed, face down on the pillow.

How could I get out of this? My lie was driving me insane.

And suddenly I saw the cellar.

Dark. Welcoming.

And forgotten.

3

It was nice and warm in the cellar. There was a small bathroom with damp patches on the wall. The toilet didn't flush but by filling up the bucket from the sink I could empty it.

I spent the rest of the morning on the bed reading *Salem's Lot* and sleeping. I snapped off half a bar of chocolate for lunch.

I was a survivor of an alien invasion. The human race had been exterminated and only a handful had managed to save themselves by hiding out in cellars or basements. I was the only one still alive in Rome. To get out I had to wait for the aliens to go back to their planet. And this, for a reason unknown to me, would happen in a week's time.

I pulled my clothes and two containers of fake tan out of my backpack. I put my sunglasses and hat on and sprayed the lotion over my face and hands.

Then, greasy all over, I climbed up onto the

chest of drawers and placed my mobile on the window sill, where it managed to get two bars of reception.

I opened a jar of artichokes in oil and polished off five.

Oh yes, this was a real holiday, much better than Cortina.

The sound of the phone ringing woke me up from a dreamless slumber.

The cellar was dark. I felt my way to the phone and, balancing on a big box, I tried to put on a cheerful voice. 'Mum!'

'So how's it going?'

'Great!'

'Where are you?'

What time was it? I looked at the display on the mobile. Eight-thirty. I had slept for ages.

'I'm at the pizzeria.'

'Ah . . .which one?'

'On the main street . . .' I couldn't remember the name of the pizzeria where we always went to eat with Grandma.

'La Pedavena?'

'Exactly.'

'How was the trip?'

'Perfect.'

'And how's the weather?'

'Lovely . . .' Maybe I was exaggerating. 'Nice. Not too bad.'

'Snow?'

How much snow could there be? 'There's a bit.'

'Is everything all right? You sound a little weird.'

'No. No. Everything's fine.'

'Put Alessia's mum on so that I can say hello.'

'She's not here. It's just us. Alessia's mum's at home.'

Silence. 'Ah . . . Tomorrow I'll call you and you put her on. Or else get her to call me.'

'Okay. I have to go now though, the pizzas are here.' And then turning to an imaginary waiter, 'That's mine . . . Mine's the one with the prosciutto.'

'All right. I'll call you tomorrow. Don't forget to wash.'

'Bye.'

'Bye, darling. Have fun.'

It hadn't gone too badly – I'd pulled it off.

Feeling satisfied, I turned on the PlayStation to play Soul Reaver for a bit. But I kept thinking back to the phone call. Mum wouldn't let up. I knew her too well. If she didn't get to speak to Alessia's mother she was capable of driving up to Cortina. And what if I told her that Mrs Roncato had broken her leg while she was skiing and was in hospital? No, I had to find something better. Nothing came to mind at the moment though.

The smell of dampness was beginning to bother me. I opened the window. My head just fitted through the bars.

Mrs Barattieri's garden was covered in a carpet of rotting leaves. A street-lamp cast a cold light that fell on the ivy-covered gate. I could see the courtyard beyond the lawn. My father's Mercedes wasn't there. He must have gone out for dinner or to play bridge.

I went back to bed.

Mum was three floors above me. She was probably lying on the settee with the Dachshunds curled up on her feet, a tray of milk and sponge cake on the coffee table. She would fall asleep there, watching a black and white film. And my father, when he got home, would wake her up and take her to bed.

I put my headphones on and Lucio Battisti began singing 'Ancora tu', 'You again'. I took them back off.

I hated that song.

4

The last time I'd heard 'Ancora tu' I was in the car with Mum. We were stuck in traffic on Corso Vittorio. A group of demonstrators had taken over Piazza Venezia, and like heat the traffic jam had expanded, paralysing the streets throughout the whole city centre.

I had spent the morning in my mother's art gallery helping her to hang some pictures by a French artist whose exhibition she would launch the following week. I liked the huge photographs of people eating alone in crowded restaurants.

Scooters slalomed between the cars. A homeless man was sleeping on the steps of a church, huddled up in a grimy sleeping bag. Rubbish bags were wrapped around his head. He looked like an Egyptian mummy.

'Come on! What's going on?' My mum pushed hard on the car horn. 'This city is becoming unbearable . . . Would you like to live in the country?'

'Where?'

'I don't know . . . Tuscany, maybe?'

'Just us two?'

'Dad would come up on the weekends.'

'And what if we bought a house in Komodo?'

'Where's Komodo?'

'It's a faraway island.'

'And why would we go and live there?'

'They have Komodo dragons. They're these huge lizards that can even eat a live goat. And they run really fast. We could train them. And use them to defend ourselves.'

'From whom?'

'From everyone.'

My mother smiled and turned up the volume of the car radio and she began singing along to Lucio Battisti: '*Ancora tu. It's no surprise, you know . . .*'

I began singing along too and when we came to the verse: '*Amore mio, have you already eaten? I'm hungry too and not just for you,*' I took her hand like a forlorn lover.

My mother laughed and shook her head. 'You're silly . . . you're silly . . .'

I realised that I was happy. The world was

outside the car windows, and Mum and I were in a traffic bubble. There was no more school, not even homework or those billions of things I should be doing to become an adult.

But suddenly my mother turned down the radio. 'Look at that dress in the window. What do you think?'

'Nice. Maybe a little too saucy?'

She looked at me in surprise. 'Saucy?! Since when have you used that word?'

'I heard it in a film. There was this woman and they said she was wearing a dress that looked saucy.'

'Do you know what it means though?'

'Of course,' I said. 'That it's too revealing.'

'I don't think it's too revealing.'

'Maybe not.'

'Shall I try it on?'

'Sure.'

And just like magic, a four-wheel drive pulled out of a free parking space in front of us. With an instinctive swerve my mother pulled in.

A loud thump against the car. Mum hit the brake and let go of the clutch. I lurched forward but the seatbelt held me back against the seat. The engine hiccupped and died.

I turned my head. A yellow Smart car was glued to the back door of the BMW.

It had driven into us.

'Noooo. What a pain!' my mother huffed as she wound down the window to inspect the damage.

I stuck my head out too. There wasn't a scratch on the BMW or anything on the bulldog-shaped nose of the Smart car. On the dashboard lay a white and light blue stuffed centipede with LAZIO written on it. Then I noticed that the Smart car was missing its left wing mirror. In the spot where it used to be was a hole, with multicoloured wires sticking out. 'Look, Mum.'

The car door flew open and spat out the trunk of a man who had to be at least six feet tall and three feet wide.

I wondered how he managed to fit into that tin can. He looked like a hermit crab stretching its head and its pincers out of its shell. He had small blue eyes, a big raven-black fringe, a horsy set of teeth and a cocoa tan.

'What happened?' my mother asked him.

The guy got out and knelt down next to the mirror. He was looking at it with a pained yet dignified expression, as if what lay on the ground wasn't a piece of plastic and glass, but the body of his mother. He didn't even touch it, like it was a corpse waiting for forensics to show up.

'What happened?' my mother said again, calmly, sticking her head out of the window.

The guy didn't even turn around, but answered, 'What happened?! You want to know what happened?' He had a deep, hoarse voice, like he was talking through a plastic pipe. 'Then get out of that car and take a look.'

'Stay here,' Mum said to me, looking me in the eye. She undid her seatbelt and got out of the car.

Through the window I saw her peach-coloured suit become flecked with rain.

A couple of pedestrians, standing beneath their umbrellas, stopped to watch. Cars were honking, trying to get around the obstacle like ants faced with a pine cone. About thirty metres away a bus began sounding its horn.

From inside the car I could see everyone's eyes settling on my mother. I started sweating and felt my breathing quicken.

'Maybe we should move,' my mother suggested to the guy. 'You know, the traffic . . .'

But the guy couldn't hear her, he kept staring at the mirror as if by the power of his mind he could join it back to the car.

So my mother moved towards him and, looking a little guilty and pretending to sympathise, she asked him again, 'How did it happen?'

The rain mixing with his hair gel had made the man's head shiny, highlighting a little bald patch right in the middle of his head.

Not having got an answer, my mother added softly, 'Is it serious?'

Finally the guy turned his head and realised that the perpetrator of the horror before him was standing next to him. He studied mum from her feet up to her hair, then he took one look at our car and a little smile appeared on his face.

The same mean little smile that Varaldi and Riccardelli had when they looked at me from their scooters. The little smile of the predator that has locked on to his prey.

I had to warn her.

The Lazio supporter had picked up the mirror like it was a robin with a broken wing. 'Maybe it's not serious for you. For me it is. I just picked my car up from the garage. Do you know how much this mirror costs?'

My mother shook her head. 'A lot?'

I was running my hands through my hair. She shouldn't play around with this guy. She had to apologise. Give him the money and end of story.

'A quarter of a waiter's pay. But what would you know? You don't have that kind of problem.'

I had to get up, out of the car, take her by the hand and run away, but I was about to faint.

My mother was shaking her head in dismay. 'Look, you were the one who drove into me . . . It's your fault.'

I saw the Lazio supporter hesitate slightly, close and open his eyes as if he were absorbing the blow he'd just been dealt. His nostrils were flaring like a truffle hound's. 'My fault? Whose? Mine? I drove into you?' Then he stood up, threw his arms wide open and grunted. 'What the fuck are you saying, bitch?'

He had called my mother a bitch.

I tried to undo my seatbelt but my hands were tingling like they'd fallen asleep.

Mum was trying to look confident. She had got straight out of the car, in the rain, polite, prepared to accept the responsibility, if necessary. She had done nothing wrong and some guy that she had never seen before had just called her a bitch.

'Bitch. Bitch. Bitch.' I repeated it to myself three times, tasting the painful scorn of that word. No kindness, no politeness, no respect, nothing.

I had to kill him.

But where had my rage gone? The red blood that filled me up whenever somebody annoyed me? The fury that set me off like a raging bull? I was a flat battery. Overcome with fear, I wasn't even able to undo my seatbelt.

'Why? What did I do?' my mother said as if she had been punched in the chest. She staggered and put her hand to her chest.

'Honey? Sweetie?' The round face of a tubby, curly-haired girl poked out of the Smart car window, wearing green sunglasses and purple lipstick. I hadn't even noticed her. 'Darling, you know what you are? You're just a bitch in a BMW. You drove into us. We saw the spot before you.'

The Lazio supporter had begun to point at Mum with his hand out flat. 'Just because you're a skinny bitch loaded with cash you think you can do whatever the fuck you want. The world is yours for the taking, isn't it?'

Curlytop began clapping her hands from inside the Smart car. 'Good on you, Teodoro. Give this slut a piece of your mind.'

I had to react, but all I could think about was that his name was Teodoro and I didn't know anyone who was called that.

I breathed, trying to push that stupid thought out of my mind. My ears and my neck were now boiling hot and my head was spinning.

Maybe Teo, the old cocker spaniel that belonged to the woman on the first floor, was actually called Teodoro.

I had to get out of there straight away. I had nothing to do with this. I had told her that the dress was saucy and if she had listened to me . . .

I undid my seatbelt, but I still couldn't move.

I was sitting on a huge giant made of stone that was hugging me and wouldn't let me go.

I looked towards the pavement hoping that someone would help us. The passers-by were a swarm of fuzzy silhouettes.

The Lazio supporter grabbed my mother by

the wrist and yanked her. 'Come and have a look, sweetheart. Come and see what you did.'

Mum lost her balance and fell over.

The high-pitched squeal of the woman: 'Teo! Teo! Leave her alone. It's late. She doesn't understand anyway. Stuck-up cow.'

My mother lay on the cobbles, one of her stockings laddered. On the cobbles covered in who knows what. They don't clean the streets in Rome. Infected pigeon shit. She was lying next to the wheel of the car, the guy towering above her.

He'll spit on her now, I thought. But all he said was, 'And you better thank God that you're a woman. Otherwise . . .'

Otherwise what would he have done to her if she weren't a woman?

Mum closed her eyes and I felt the giant squeezing me in his stone arms, taking away my breath, and then he jumped through the roof of our car and he and I flew over the people, over the Lazio supporter, over my mother sprawled on the cobbles, over the traffic, over the roofs lined with crows, past the church steeples.

And I fainted.

5

At nine o'clock the sun pierced the dirty windows with rays of gold. Maybe it was because of the heat the hot water pipes gave off, but it was hard to stay awake down here.

I yawned and in my pants and T-shirt went into the bathroom to brush my teeth.

My armpits were holding up for now. I wasn't crazy about the idea of washing myself with cold water and, besides, it didn't matter if I stank. Who was going to get a whiff of me anyway? I sprayed myself with the fake tan and made myself a Nutella sandwich.

I decided to spend a couple of hours exploring the cellar. All this stuff belonged to the previous owner of our flat, Countess Nunziante, who had died without relatives. My father had bought the house with all her furniture and stuff in it and stacked everything up down here.

Inside the drawers of an old mahogany chest I found brightly-coloured clothes, notebooks full of accounting, solved crossword puzzles, and boxes full of staples, paperclips, fountain pens, transparent stones, packets of Muratti cigarettes, empty perfume bottles and dried-up lipsticks. There were also packs of postcards. Cannes, Viareggio, Ischia, Madrid. Tarnished silver cutlery. Spectacles. I even found a blonde wig, which I popped on my head, and then I slipped into an orange silk dressing gown. I began moving through the cellar as if it were the reception hall of a castle. 'Good evening, Duke, I am the Countess Nunziante. Ah, Countess Sinibaldi is here too. Yes, this party is a little dull. And I still haven't seen the Marquis de Monkey. He hasn't ended up in the crocodile pit, has he?'

Beneath a pile of furniture was a long chest painted with red and green flowers. It looked like a coffin.

'Here lies poor Goffredo. He ate a poisoned veal cutlet.'

My mobile began ringing.

I snorted. 'No way! Fucking hell! Mum, please. Leave me alone.'

I tried to ignore it but I couldn't. At last I couldn't take it any more and I climbed up to the window. The display showed a number I didn't know. Who was it? Apart from Mum, Nihal, Grandma and, on occasion, Dad, nobody called me. I stood there staring at the phone, not sure what to do. In the end, I was too curious not to answer. 'Hello?'

'Hello, Lorenzo. It's Olivia.'

It took me a couple of seconds to work out it was that Olivia . . . Olivia, my half-sister. 'Oh. Hi . . .'

'How are you?'

'Well, thanks, and you?'

'Well. Sorry if I'm interrupting you. I got your number from Aunt Roberta. Listen, I wanted to ask you something. Do you know if your mother and Dad are at home?'

It's a trap!

I had to be careful. Maybe Mum had suspected something and was using Olivia to work out where I really was. But Olivia and Mum, as far as I knew, didn't talk to each other. 'I don't know . . . I'm away for ski week.'

'Oh . . .' Her voice was disappointed. 'Well, you must be having fun.'

'Yes.'

67

'Tell me something, Lorenzo. Are your parents normally in at this time?'

What sort of a question was that? 'Dad's at work. And Mum sometimes goes to the gym or to the gallery. It depends.'

Silence. 'Okay. And if they're not there, is anyone else in?'

'Nihal will be.'

'Who's Nihal?'

'The housekeeper.'

'Ah. Well. Listen, can you do me a favour?'

'Sure.'

'Don't tell anyone I called.'

'Okay.'

'Promise me you won't.'

'I promise I won't.'

'Good boy. Have fun skiing. Is there much snow?'

'A bit.'

'Well, bye then. And don't forget, not a word.'

'Yeah. Bye.' I hung up and took off the wig, trying to work out what the hell she wanted from me. And why did she want to know if Mum and Dad were at home? Why didn't she just call them? I shrugged my shoulders. It was none of my business. In any case, if it was a trap, I hadn't been fooled.

The only time I'd seen my half-sister Olivia was at Easter in 1998.

I was twelve and she was twenty-one. The times before that didn't count. We had spent a couple of summers together in Capri at Grandma Laura's house, but I was too little to remember.

Olivia was the daughter of my father and some woman from Como who my mum hated. A dentist whom my father had married before I was born. Back then he lived in Milan with the dentist and he had had Olivia. Then they'd divorced and Dad had married Mum.

My father didn't speak easily about his daughter. Every now and then he would go and visit her and he always came back in a bad mood. From what I could understand Olivia was crazy. She pretended to be a photographer but she just got into trouble. She'd failed her high-school exams and run away from home a couple of times, and then in Paris she'd had an affair with Faustini, my father's accountant.

I had worked all these things out in bits and

pieces because my parents didn't discuss Olivia in front of me. But sometimes, in the car, they would forget I was there and so I was able to pick up snippets.

Two days before Easter we had gone to visit my uncle who lives in Campagnano. During the ride there Dad had told Mum that he'd invited Olivia for lunch to convince her to go to Sicily. There were priests there and they would keep her in a nice place with fruit trees, orchards and things to do.

I had expected Olivia to be ugly and with an unpleasant face like Cinderella's stepsisters. Instead she was incredibly beautiful, one of those girls that as soon as you look at them your face burns red and everybody knows you think she is beautiful, and if she talks to you, you don't know what to do with your hands, you don't even know how to sit down. She had lots of curly blonde hair that fell all the way down her back and grey eyes, and she was sprinkled with freckles, just like me. She was tall and had big, wide breasts. She could have been the queen of a medieval kingdom.

She had barely spoken during dinner. Afterwards

she and Dad had locked themselves in the study.
She left without saying goodbye to anyone.

I stood there for a while thinking about that
strange phone call, then I realised that I had a
much more serious problem to solve. If I had
another Sim card I could send a text to my mother
pretending to be Alessia's mother. But it wouldn't
work. Mum wanted to talk to her.

I put on a high-pitched voice: 'Greetings,
Signora, this is . . . Alessia's mother . . . I wanted
to let you know that your son is fine and having
lots of fun. Goodbye.'

I was terrible. She'd have recognised me on
the spot.

I picked up the phone and wrote:

Mum we're in a hut up high in the
mountains. There's no reception.
I'll call you tomorrow. I love you.

And so I'd earned myself another day.

I turned off the phone, cleared my mind of my
mother, flopped down on the bed, put on my headphones and started playing Soul Reaver. I came up

71

against a mutant so tough I couldn't beat him, which pissed me off, so I switched off the PlayStation and made myself a mayonnaise and mushroom sandwich.

I loved it here. If they brought me food and water I could spend the rest of my life here. And I realised that if I ever ended up in solitary confinement in prison I would be as happy as a pig in shit.

The fly had finally found a place where it could be itself, and so it may as well take a nap.

My eyes flew open suddenly.

Someone was fiddling with the lock on the door.

I had never even considered the possibility that someone might want to come into the cellar.

I stared at the door, but I couldn't move. It was as if I were stuck to the bed. My throat had closed over and I was struggling to breathe.

In an unexpected move, like I was freeing myself of a spider's web, I flung myself off the bed, banging my left knee on the corner of the bedside table. Gritting my teeth and swallowing a scream of pain, I limped towards the space between the cupboard and the wall. Grazing my legs, I slipped under a table, where rolls of rugs were piled up. I stretched out on top of them as the blood pulsed in my eardrums.

They wouldn't be able to unlock the door. The lock was old and if you pushed the key the whole way in, it wouldn't turn.

Then the door flew open.

I bit down on a smelly rug.

I could only see a slice of the floor from where I was. I heard footsteps and then a pair of jeans and black cowboy boots appeared.

Nihal didn't own a pair of boots. My father wore Church brogues, and moccasins in summer. My mother had lots of pairs, but none of them were that scruffy. And the Silver Monkey only had old, worn-out trainers. Who could it be?

Whoever it was would notice that the cellar was being lived in. It was all there. The bed, the food, the television turned on.

Meanwhile the black boots were wandering around the room like they were looking for something. They moved towards my bed and stopped.

The boots' owner was breathing through their mouth, like they had a cold. They lifted up a tin

73

from the table and put it back down again. 'Is anyone there?' A woman's voice.

I crushed the rug between my teeth. If she doesn't find me, I said to myself, I will go and visit my cousin Vittorio, who loves playing board games, every single day. I swear to God I'll be his best friend.

'Who's in here?'

I closed my eyes and put my hands over my ears but I could still hear her walking, moving, looking.

'Come out from under there. I can see you.'

I opened my eyes again. A shadowy figure was sitting on my bed.

'Move it.'

No, I would never move, not on my life.

'Are you deaf? Come out from under there.'

Maybe it was best to know who it was. I pulled myself up and, like a dog that has been caught with his nose in the fridge, I slid out.

Olivia was sitting on my bed.

She'd lost a lot of weight and her square cheekbones stuck out. Her face looked stretched and tired and her long blonde hair had been cut short. Above her jeans she was wearing a faded T-shirt with the Camel cigarettes logo and a blue sailor's jacket.

She wasn't as beautiful as she had been two years ago.

She studied me, perplexed. 'What are you doing here?'

If there was something I hated, it was being seen in my pants and in particular being seen by women. Embarrassed, I picked up my trousers and slipped them on.

'Why are you hiding down here?'

I didn't know what to say. I was so confused I could barely shrug my shoulders.

My stepsister got up and looked around. 'Forget about it, I don't care. I'm looking for a box that I gave to my . . . to our father. The servant, upstairs, told me that it should be down here. He couldn't come down with me because he was ironing. Was he being an idiot?'

Nihal was actually a bit of an idiot with people he didn't know well. He had this bad habit of looking down his nose at everyone.

'It's a big box, with OLIVIA written on it. Give me a hand looking for it.'

I felt so happy that my stepsister didn't care

what I was doing in there that I really did help her to look for it.

But there was no sign of the box, or rather, there were heaps of boxes but none had OLIVIA written on them.

My stepsister shook her head. 'See how little your father cares about my stuff?'

I whispered, 'He's your father too.'

'You're ri—' Olivia squeezed her hand into a victory fist. Sitting beneath a cabinet, just behind the cellar door, was a box covered in sellotape, with OLIVIA'S HOUSE FRAGILE written on it.

'Here it is. Look where he put it. Give me a hand, it's heavy.'

We dragged it into the middle of the room.

Olivia sat down and crossed her legs. She peeled the tape off and began pulling out books, CDs, clothes and make-up, throwing them on the floor. 'Here it is.'

It was a white book with a worn-out cover. *The Notebook*, *The Proof*, *The Third Lie: Three Novels.*

She began flipping through it, looking for something and talking to herself. 'Fuck, it was here. I can't believe it. That bastard Antonio must have found it.' She got up quickly. Her eyes had gone shiny. She put her hands on her hips, looked up at the ceiling and began kicking the box in a rage. 'Fucking hell! Fucking hell! I hate you. You even took that. And now what the fuck am I supposed to do?'

I stared at her terrified, but I couldn't stop myself. 'What was in there?'

I thought she was going to burst into tears.

She looked at me. 'Have you got any money?'

'What?'

'Money. I need money.'

'No, I'm sorry.' Actually I did have a bit. Dad had given me some spending money for the mountain, but I wanted to save it to buy a stereo.

'Tell me the truth.'

I shook my head and opened my arms wide. 'I swear. I don't have any.'

She studied me, trying to work out whether I was lying to her. 'Do me a favour. Put all this stuff back in the box and close it up.' She opened the cellar door. 'See you.'

I said, 'Listen.'

She stopped. 'What is it?'

'Please, don't tell anyone I'm here. Not even Nihal. If you tell them I'm dead.'

Olivia looked at me without seeing me. She was thinking about something else, something that worried her. Then she blinked as if to waken herself. 'All right. I won't tell anyone.'

'Thanks.'

'By the way, your face is orange. You overdid the fake tan.' And she closed the door.

Operation Bunker was falling apart. Mum wanted to speak to Alessia's mother. Olivia had found me. And I had a fluorescent face.

I kept looking at myself in the mirror and rereading the tanning instructions. It didn't say anything about how long it took to go away.

I found an old bottle of Jif Lemon, smeared it all over my face, and then lay down on the bed.

The only thing I was sure of was that Olivia wouldn't say anything. She didn't seem like the sort of person who would tell on me.

After ten minutes I washed my face but it was just as orange as before.

I rummaged through my sister's big box. Everything had just been chucked in, mostly clothes and shoes. An old laptop. A manual camera without a lens. A statue of Buddha made of smelly wood. Sheets of paper with stuff written on it in big round handwriting. The majority were lists. People to invite to a party. Shopping lists. In a light blue folder I found some photographs of Olivia when she was still in good shape. In one of them she was lying on a red velvet settee, wearing just a man's shirt, part of her boob was visible. In another shot she was sitting on a chair, a cigarette in her mouth, putting on her stockings. The one I liked the most was one of her taken from behind with her head turned towards the camera. With one hand she covered her boob. And her legs looked like they were never-ending.

I shouldn't even think about her. Olivia was fifty per cent my sister.

Among the photos there was a small one, in black and white. My father, with long hair, wearing jeans and a leather jacket, sitting on the bollard of a jetty with a little girl, probably Olivia, who was sitting on his knee and eating an ice cream.

I burst out laughing. I would never have imagined that when he was young my father would have dressed so badly. I'd always known him with greying hair cut short and a grey suit with a tie and the shoes with holes in them. But here, with his hair like an old-fashioned tennis player's, he looked happy.

There was even a letter that Olivia had written to Dad.

Dear Dad,

I'm writing to thank you for the money. Each time you get me out of trouble using your wealth I ask myself: if money didn't exist in this world, how would my father help me? And then I ask myself if it's the guilt or the love for me that makes you do it. You know what? I don't want to know. I have been lucky to have a father like you who lets me live my own life and who, when I make a mistake, practically always helps me out. But enough now. I don't want you to help me any more.

You've never liked me, I annoy you. When you're with me you're always too serious. Maybe it's because I'm the living proof of a relationship gone wrong and each time you think of me you're reminded of your shitty marriage to my mother. That's not my fault, though. I know that for sure. For all the other stuff, I'm not sure. Maybe if I'd tried to be in contact more often, if I'd tried to break down the wall that separates us, maybe it would all have been different.

I was thinking that if I had to write a book that tells the story of my life I would call the chapter on you 'Diary of a Hatred'. Anyhow, I have to learn not to hate you. I have to learn not to hate you when your money arrives and when you call me to find out how it's all going. I have hated you for too long, with no remorse. I'm sick and tired of it.

So thank you once again but from now on even if you feel the urge to help me out, repress it. You are the master of repression and silence.

Your daughter,
Olivia

I read it three times. I hadn't realised that Olivia hated Dad so much. I knew they didn't get on, but he was her father, after all. I mean, give him a break! If you didn't know Dad you might think he wasn't that nice. He looked like one of those men who takes himself too seriously, as though they carry the weight of the world on their shoulders.

But if you met him at the beach in summer or on the ski slope he would be very polite and nice. Anyway, Olivia was the one who had decided not to see him any more. She was the nasty one who had ganged up on him with the dentist. Dad was doing his best to rebuild their relationship.

"'Diary of a Hatred" . . . That's crazy. And what does she need all that money for anyway?' I said. I'd done the right thing not giving her mine. She didn't deserve it. And she'd even had photos taken in the nude.

I threw all the stuff back inside the box and put it back behind the door.

It must have been about three a.m. and I was floating in the dark, headphones on, playing Soul Reaver, when I had the feeling that there had been a noise in the cellar. I took the headphones off and slowly turned my head.

Someone was knocking at the window.

I jumped backwards and a tingle slid down my spine like I had hairs on my back and somebody was caressing them. I swallowed a scream.

Who could it be?

Whoever it was wouldn't stop knocking.

The windows reflected the bluish glare of the TV screen and me, standing up, terrified.

I tried to swallow. My head was spinning in fear. Inhaling and exhaling, I had to keep calm. There was no danger. There were bars on the window and nobody could slip through them.

I turned on the torch and shakily pointed it at the window.

Behind the glass Olivia was gesturing to me to open up.

'Fuck!' I snorted. I went to the window and threw it open. Icy air slipped in. 'What do you want now?'

Her eyes were red and she looked really tired. 'Fuck. I was knocking for half an hour.'

'I had my headphones on. What is it?'

'I need hospitality, little brother.'

I pretended I didn't understand. 'What do you mean?'

'I mean that I don't have anywhere to sleep.'

'And you want to sleep here?'

'Well done.'

I shook my head. 'No way.'

'Why?'

'Because. This is my cellar. I'm here. There's only room for one person.'

She looked at me in silence, like she thought I was joking.

'I'm sorry, that's the way it is. I really can't . . .'

She shook her head disbelievingly. 'It's freezing cold. It must be minus five out here. I don't know where the fuck to go. I'm asking you a favour.'

'I'm sorry.'

'You know what? You're your father's son.'

'Our father,' I corrected.

She pulled out a packet of Marlboro and lit one. 'Can you explain to me why I can't stay here tonight? What's the problem?'

What should I say to her? I was getting really angry. I could feel it pushing up against my diaphragm. 'You'll mess everything up. There isn't any room. It's dangerous. I'm here undercover. I can't open the door for you. Go somewhere else. In fact, I've got an idea. Ring the buzzer upstairs. They'll put you up in the guest room. You'll be much more comfortable . . .'

'I'd rather sleep on a park bench in Villa Borghese than sleep with those two tossers.'

Who did she think she was? What had Dad done to deserve such a daughter? I kicked the wall. 'Please . . . I'm begging you . . . everything is just perfect in here. I've organised everything and now you arrive and mess it all up . . .' I realised I had started to whine and I hated whining.

'All right . . . What's your name? Lorenzo. Lorenzo, listen carefully. I've been good to you. This morning you asked me not to say anything and I didn't say anything. I didn't ask you anything. I don't want to know. That's your business. I am asking you a favour. If you come out for just a moment and open the main door I'll come in. Nobody will see us.'

'No. I swore I wouldn't come out.'

She looked at me. 'Who did you swear that to?'

'To myself.'

She took a drag of her cigarette. 'Fine. You know what I'll do? I'll start ringing the buzzer and I'll tell them you're down in the cellar. What do you think of that?'

'You wouldn't . . .'

A smug little smile came appeared on her face. 'You don't think so? You don't know me . . .' She moved towards the middle of the garden and in a fairly loud voice said, 'Listen up, everyone! Can you hear me? A boy is hiding in the cellar. It's

Lorenzo Cuni, who's pretending to be away on ski week . . . Hello . . .'

I threw my arms against the bars and I begged, 'Shut up! Shut up, please.'

She looked at me in amusement. 'So, are you going to let me in or do I have to wake up the whole building?'

I couldn't believe how sly she was. She'd completely fucked me over. 'All right, but you have to leave tomorrow morning. Promise?'

'I promise.'

'I'm coming. Go round to the main door.'

I ran out in such a rush that I only noticed when I was halfway along the corridor that I wasn't wearing shoes. I had to be super-quick. Luckily it was late. My parents were often out in the evening, but not until three in the morning.

Imagine if when I open the main door I run straight into my parents on their way in. I would look so stupid, I thought as I jumped up the stairs two at a time and dodged past the porter's flat. At night there was no need to worry about the Silver Monkey. His wasn't sleep but a sort of hibernation, he'd explained to me, and his disrupted sleeping pattern was all the fault of the gypsies.

One night, about three years ago, they had entered his house and sprayed an anaesthetic in his face. With all the houses nearby full of money, paintings and jewellery those morons had broken into the Silver Monkey's flat. They took a pair of binoculars and a radio. Anyway, the poor guy had slept for three days straight. They hadn't even been able to keep him awake in the hospital emergency ward. He explained to me that since that night he always felt sleepy and when he did go to bed he slept so deeply that 'if an earthquake hits, I'm fucked. What the hell did those gypsy bastards spray me with?'

I crossed the foyer. The marble was cold beneath my feet.

I opened the main door and she was standing there, waiting for me.

'Thanks, little brother,' she said.

6

Olivia sat down on the settee. She took off her boots, crossed her legs and lit up another cigarette. 'It really is a nice little spot here. Very cosy.'

'Thanks,' I answered as if it were my house.

'Have you got anything to drink?'

'There's some fruit juice, some warm Coke and water.'

'Don't you have any beer?'

'No.'

'Some juice then.' She ordered as if she were in a café.

I brought her the bottle and she took a big swig and wiped her mouth on the sleeve of her cardigan. 'This is the first quiet moment of my day.' She rubbed her eyes and puffed out a cloud of smoke. 'I need to rest.' She let her head fall back against the settee and sat there, just staring at the ceiling.

I watched her silently not knowing what to say. Maybe she didn't feel like talking, or she didn't consider me someone she could chat with. So much the better.

I lay down and began reading, but I couldn't concentrate. I studied her from behind the book. She had the cigarette in her mouth and her eyes were closed. The ash was growing longer but she didn't tap it off. I was worried that it would fall on her and burn her. Maybe she was sleeping.

'Are you cold? Do you want a blanket?' I asked her just to see.

It took her ages to answer me. With her eyes closed she said, 'Yes, thank you.'

'These are the Countess's . . . They're old and they smell a bit.'

'The Countess?'

'Yeah, she lived in the house before we did. Seems like Dad bought the house and he didn't even kick her out. He waited for her to die. To give her a hand. All this stuff is from her house.'

'Ah. He bought the residual life estate.'

'What?'

'You don't know what residual life estate is?'

'No.'

'It's when someone who doesn't have any relatives or any more money sells their house below market value, but can go on living there until they die . . . It's not easy to explain.' She laughed to herself. 'Wait. I'll explain it better . . .' She was speaking slowly, like she couldn't find the words. 'Imagine you're old and you've got nobody, and you get fuck all from your pension. So what do you do? You sell your house with you in it and then when you die the house and everything in it goes to the person who bought it . . . Get it now?'

'Yes.' I hadn't understood. 'For how long, though?'

'It depends when you die. A day or ten years. You might sell the residual life estate and live for another twenty years.'

'How come?'

'I don't know . . . But I think that if people are hoping you'll die . . .'

'So if you buy the house you hope the old lady dies quickly? That's not nice.'

'Clever boy. So Dad . . . bought your . . . house when the . . .' And she stopped. I waited for her to finish but I saw that her arms had flopped to the side like she'd been shot in the chest. The cigarette, hanging from her lips, had burned itself out, and the ashes had fallen onto her neck.

I crept towards her and put my ear up against her face. She was breathing.

I took the stub out of her mouth and then I got a blanket and put it over her.

When I woke the sun was already high in a blue cloudless sky. The palm tree shook, moved by the wind. It was a perfect day for skiing in Cortina.

Olivia was curled up on the settee and was sleeping with her face squashed up against a grubby cushion. She must have been really tired.

'Let's leave her be a little longer,' I said to myself and I remembered my mobile was turned off. As soon as I turned it on I got three texts. Two from my mother. She was worried and wanted me to call her as soon as we reached a place where there was reception. One from my father. It said that Mum was worried and to call her as soon as I had reception again.

I had breakfast and then I settled down to play Soul Reaver.

Olivia woke up an hour later.

I kept playing but every now and then I sneaked a look at her. I wanted to make it clear to her that I was tough, someone who didn't need anyone.

She looked liked she'd been chewed up and spat out by a monster who had found her too bitter to eat. It took her half an hour to sit up. She had cushion marks on her cheek and forehead. She kept rubbing her eyes and moving her tongue around inside her mouth. Finally she let out one word: 'Water.'

I brought some to her. She put the bottle to her mouth and drank deeply. Then, wincing, she began touching her arms and her legs. 'Everything hurts. It's like I've got barbed wire inside my muscles.'

I put my hands up. 'You must have got the flu. I don't have any medicine here. You should go to the chemist. If you go to the square . . .'

'I haven't got the strength to leave.'

'What? You promised you'd leave this morning.'

Olivia rubbed her hand across her forehead. 'Is this how they brought you up? They've taught you to be a complete wanker. Although it's not just about upbringing – there must be something twisted and wrong inside of you.'

I didn't speak. I kept my head down, unable to answer. What the hell did she want from me? She wasn't even my sister. I didn't know her. I didn't annoy anyone, so why did she have to annoy me? She had come into my den under false pretences and now she didn't want to leave.

She struggled to stand up, then she got down on her knees with a grimace of pain and looked straight at me. Her pupils were so wide and black that the grey of her irises was hardly noticeable. 'Look, if you stay hidden away in here, minding your own business, it doesn't mean that you're a good person. It's just a cop-out.'

It was as if she had read my mind.

'I'm sorry . . . There's not enough food for both of us. That's the only reason. And you have to be quiet here. And then . . . No. No way. I have to stay here by myself,' I stammered, squeezing my hands into fists.

She put her hands up as if she surrendered. 'Fine, I'll leave. You're a real wanker.'

'Exactly.'

'And you're out of your mind.'

'Exactly.'

'And you stink.'

I sniffed under my arm. 'What do I care? I can stink as much as I want. And look who's talking. You stink too . . .'

Right then the phone rang.

It was my mother.

I pretended I couldn't hear it, hoping it would stop, but it didn't.

Olivia looked at me. 'What? Are you not going to answer it?'

'No.'

'Why not?'

'Because.'

It didn't stop. Mum must be really angry. I could see her, sitting on her bed, huffing and puffing. I snapped into action, jumping over the furniture to reach the phone. I answered. 'Mum.'

'Lorenzo. Is everything okay?'

'Yes.'

'I've called you a hundred times.'

'Did you not get my text?'

'Did you think that was enough? You should have called me before you went up to the mountain.'

'I know . . . I'm sorry, but we decided at the very last minute. I was just about to call you.'

'You had me worried. How are you?'

'Fine. Just fine.'

'I have to talk to Alessia's mother.'

'She can't talk now. Call back later.'

She was silent for a second, then she blew up. 'That's it, Lorenzo. You either let me speak to Alessia's mother or I'll call the other kids' parents.' Her voice was hard and she was holding back from yelling. 'I've had enough of this story. What are you hiding from me?'

She had me cornered. I couldn't get away with it any more. I looked at Olivia. 'Here she is . . . Hang on while I go and get her. I'll see if she can come to the phone.' I put the phone down and I got off the window sill. I sat down next to Olivia and whispered in her ear, 'Please, you have to help me . . . I'm begging you. You have to pretend to be Alessia's mother. Mum thinks I'm skiing in Cortina with this girl called Alessia Roncato who invited me there for ski week. You have to pretend to be Alessia's mother. Tell her I'm fine and that everything's going fine. Oh, and it's really important you tell her that I'm nice.'

A wicked smile curved my half-sister's mouth. 'No chance . . .'

'Please.'

'I'd rather die.'

I took her by the wrist. 'If she finds out I

96

haven't gone skiing I'm dead. They'll send me to the psychologist again.'

She shook herself free of my grip. 'No way . . . No way am I helping out a selfish little shit who's kicking me out of his flea-ridden cellar.'

What a bitch. She'd fucked me over again.

'Okay, fine. If you talk to her, you can stay.'

She picked up her boots. 'Who says I want to stay here?'

'I swear I'll do anything you want.'

'On your knees.' And she pointed to the floor.

'On my knees?'

'On your knees.'

I obeyed.

'Repeat. I swear on my parents' lives that I will be Olivia Cuni's slave . . .'

'Come on, she's still on the phone . . . Go on,' I whimpered in distress.

She was calm. 'Say it.'

She was killing me. 'I swear on my parents' lives that I will be Olivia Cuni's slave . . .'

'For the rest of my life . . .'

'For the rest of my life?! Are you crazy?' I looked up at the ceiling and snorted. 'For the rest of my life.'

'And I will always be kind and generous to her.'

'And I will always be kind and generous to her. Now, please . . .'

She got up, wincing with pain. 'Does your mother know this woman?'

'No.'

'What's the daughter's name?'

'Alessia. Alessia Roncato.'

She walked like an old arthritic woman and it was a struggle for her to reach the window. She must really not have been well. But when she spoke her voice was bright. 'Hello, Mrs Cuni! Good morning. How is everything?'

I began biting my hand in anxiety.

She sounded so happy to be speaking to my mother.

'Of course . . . of course . . . Yes, of course. Lorenzo told me. Please forgive me for not having called you myself . . . No, it's my fault, but we've just been so busy. You know how things are up in the mountains . . . My pleasure . . . My pleasure . . . Thank you, it's been a pleasure to have him with us. He's such a well-behaved boy . . . Of course. Anyhow, everything is fine. Snow? Is there much snow?' She looked at me unsure of what to say.

'A bit,' I suggested in a whisper.

'A bit,' she said calmly. 'Alessia is so happy.' She looked at me and shook her head. 'Your son, if I may say so, is very funny. He makes us all laugh. It's a real pleasure to have him with us. He's such a generous young man.'

'Fantastic. You're a star,' I said, without even realising I was talking out loud.

'I'm happy to leave you my mobile phone number. Anyhow, we'll call you again. Take care . . . You have a nice day too. Bye . . . Of course . . . Thank you. Thanks.' And she hung up.

I jumped with my arms up in the air. 'Hooray! You're a star. You were exactly like Alessia's mother. Do you know her?'

'I know her sort,' she said and slumped against the wall, squeezed her eyes shut, opened them again, and then she looked at me and vomited into her hands.

She kept on vomiting in the bathroom. Or rather, she tried to, but wasn't able. Then she flopped down on the settee exhausted and took her trousers off. Her white legs trembled and kicked the air like they were trying to free themselves of the trembling. 'Here it comes. Fuck, it's here . . .' she panted with her eyes closed.

What sort of illness did she have? What if it were contagious?

'What's up?'

'Nothing . . . It's nothing.'

'What's the matter with you? Is this illness catching?'

'No. You don't need to worry. Leave me alone. Just mind your own business like I'm not here. All right?'

I swallowed. 'All right.'

She had malaria. Like Caravaggio.

She'd told me to mind my own business. Perfect. No problem. I was a master at doing that. I settled down to play Soul Reaver. I was still struggling to beat that same old mutant. Every now and then I couldn't help stealing a look at her.

She couldn't keep still for more than a minute. She was distressed, constantly changing position like she was lying on a carpet of broken bottles. She wrapped herself in the blanket then threw it off and fidgeted and flinched like somebody was torturing her.

It was driving me crazy the way she was doing these over-the-top groans. It sounded like she was faking it just to annoy me.

I put my headphones on and turned the volume all the way up, rolled over and faced the wall and stuck my head so deeply inside my book that I went cross-eyed. I read a couple of lines and then I closed my eyes.

I opened them two hours later. Olivia was sitting on the edge of the settee, all sweaty, jiggling her legs anxiously and staring at the floor. She had taken her cardigan off. She was wearing a saggy, dark blue vest and you could see her boobs hanging down. She was so thin, all bones, with long narrow feet, a thin neck like a greyhound and wide shoulders, and her arms . . .

What did she have in the middle of her arms?

Purple spots studded with little red dots.

She lifted her head up. 'You slept, didn't you?'

That place in Sicily where Dad wanted to send her . . .

'What?'

The money . . .

'Did you sleep?'

The way my parents stopped talking about Olivia as soon as they saw me . . .

'Yes . . .'

The illness that wasn't catching.

'I have to eat something . . .'

She was like those people in Villa Borghese. Those people who sit on the benches. Those people who ask you if you have any change. Those people with beers. I kept away from them. They'd always scared me.

'Can you give me a biscuit? A bit of bread?'

And now one of them was here.

I got up and took the bag of sliced bread over to her.

They were next to me. Inside my den.

She threw the bread down on the settee. 'I want to wash . . . I disgust myself.'

'There's only cold water.' I was surprised that I'd managed to answer.

'Doesn't matter. I have to do something, take control,' she said to herself. She struggled to stand and went into the bathroom.

I waited to hear the water running and then I leapt to her backpack. Inside was a worn-out purse, a diary full of scraps of paper, her mobile phone – and some syringes wrapped in plastic.

7

I lay on the bed, staring at the ceiling. It was quiet, but if I stopped breathing I could hear Olivia in the bathroom, the cars passing on the street, the sweeping of the Silver Monkey's broom in the court-yard, a phone ringing off in the distance, the pilot light in the boiler. And the smell of all that stuff piled up, the sharp, pungent smell of wooden furniture and damp rugs.

A thud.

I lifted my head up off the pillow.

The bathroom door was ajar.

I got up and went to see.

Olivia was on the floor, naked, white, bent over between the toilet and the basin, trying to get up but unable to do so. Her legs kept slipping on the wet tiles like a horse on ice. She had only a few hairs on her pussy.

I stood there staring at her.

She looked like a zombie. A zombie who has just been shot.

She saw me, standing there next to the door jamb and ground her teeth. 'Get out! Get out of here! Shut that fucking door!'

I went over to get Countess Nunziante's dressing gown and hung it on the doorknob for her. When she came out, wrapped in a filthy towel, she grabbed it, stared at it, slipped it on and then lay down on the settee. Without saying a word she turned her back to me.

I put my headphones on. One of Dad's CDs was on. It was a piece for piano which lasted forever, so calm and repetitive that it made me feel far away, on the other side of a screen, like I was watching a documentary. Olivia and I weren't in the same room.

My sister got worse and worse. She trembled like she had a temperature. She was a jetty against which waves of pain washed up. She kept her eyes closed, but she wasn't sleeping. I could hear her whining to herself. 'Fuck off. What a fucking pain. I can't take this anymore . . . I just can't take any more.'

The unchanging music kept beating away in my ears while my sister got up from the settee then lay back down again. She scratched her legs till they bled. She got up again, she fretted, she rested her head against the cupboard door, her face pulled tight in pain. She began inhaling and exhaling with her hands on her hips. 'Come on, Oli, you can do it . . . Come on, come on, for fuck's sake.' Then she curled up on her side with her hands pressed up against her face. She stayed like that for ages.

I breathed a sigh of relief. It looked like she had fallen asleep in that uncomfortable position. But she hadn't. She got up and began kicking anything within reach.

I pulled off the headphones, got up and grabbed her by the wrist. 'You have to shut up! If you keep this up everyone will hear us! Please . . .'

She looked at me with eyes shot through with blood and hate and pushed me away. 'Please, my ass. Fuck off! Put your shitty little headphones back on. You idiot.' She kicked the porcelain dog, which fell over and smashed.

I begged. 'Please . . . please . . . Don't be like this . . . We'll both be in trouble if you carry on like this. Don't you get it?'

'Get away. I swear to God I'm going to kill you.' She shoved me against a glass lampshade, which shattered.

A blind rage engulfed me. My muscles tensed, and as though I were about to explode I screamed, 'No, I'm going to kill you!' And lowering my head I ran into her. 'You have to leave me alone! Don't you get it?' I stretched out my arms and pushed her roughly.

Olivia flew backwards, tripped and banged her shoulder into the cupboard. She didn't move, her mouth open, unbelieving.

'What do you want from me? Get out!' I growled.

Olivia moved closer and slapped me. 'Bastard . . . You have no right.'

I'm going to kill her now, I thought, touching my flaming hot cheek. I felt a burning lump in my throat. I held back my tears, made two fists and jumped on her. 'Get out, you fucking junkie.'

We ended up on the settee. I was on top, she was underneath. Olivia kicked her legs and slammed her fists in the air trying to get free of me but I was stronger than her. I grabbed her wrists and screamed at her, centimetres from her face, 'What the fuck do you want from me? Tell me!'

She tried to free herself but suddenly, as though

she had no strength left for fighting, she went limp, and I fell on top of her.

I pulled myself up and moved away. I was shaking all over, afraid of what I could have done to her. I could have killed her. I began kicking boxes to calm myself down. A shard of glass got stuck in my foot. I pulled it out and hissed in pain.

Olivia was sobbing, her face pushed up against the back of the settee and her legs held tightly by her arms.

'That's enough!' I limped over to my backpack, took the money out of the envelope and screamed, 'Here you go. Use this. Take it. As long as you get out of here.' And I threw the banknotes at her.

Olivia raised herself off the settee and picked them up off the floor. 'You little bastard . . . I knew you had some.' She grabbed her trousers, squeezed the money in her fist and closed her eyes. Tears streamed from the corners of her eyes. Her shoulders shook. 'No. I can't . . .' She let the money fall and put a hand over her face. 'I swore I would stop. And this time . . . I'm stopping . . . otherwise it's all over.'

I couldn't understand a thing. Her words mixed with her sobs.

'I'm a worthless piece of shit . . . I did . . . it . . . I did it . . . How could I?' She looked at me and took my hand. 'I fucking had sex with a disgusting pervert just to buy a hit. He fucked me in a car park. Go on, say it, say I'm worthless . . . Say it, say it . . . Please . . .' She collapsed on the floor and she began groaning like she'd been punched in the stomach.

She's not breathing, I thought, covering my ears, but her groans pierced my eardrums.

Someone has to help her. Someone has to come here. Otherwise she'll die.

'Please . . . please . . . help me,' I begged the walls of the room.

Then I saw her.

Lying on the floor surrounded by the money, alone and desperate.

Something inside me snapped. The giant that had been holding me up against his stone chest had let me go.

'I'm sorry. I didn't want to hurt you. I'm sorry . . .' I grabbed my sister by the arms and pulled her up from the floor.

She was out of breath, like she was choking. I didn't know what to do, so I shook her and patted her on the back. 'Don't die. Please. Don't die. I'm going to help you now. I'll take care of everything . . .' And little by little I heard a breath of air slide into her mouth and down her throat into her chest. Very little to begin with, then her breathing gradually grew deeper until she eventually said in a whisper, 'I'm not going to die. It takes more than that to kill me.'

I hugged her and leaned my forehead against her neck, my nose on her collarbone, and I burst into tears.

I couldn't stop. The sobs came in gusts. I would settle for a few moments and then it welled up and I cried even louder than before.

Olivia was shaking and her teeth were chattering. I wrapped her up in a blanket but she barely noticed. It looked like she was sleeping, but she wasn't asleep. She was squeezing her lips together from the pain.

I felt useless. I didn't know what to do. 'Do you feel like a sip of Coke? A sandwich?'

She didn't answer me.

And in the end I asked, 'Do you want me to call Dad?'

She opened her eyes and murmured, 'No. Please don't.'

'What can I do then?'

'Do you really want to help me?'

I nodded.

'You have to find me some sleeping pills then. I need to sleep. I can't take any more of this.'

'I've only got some aspirin, paracetamol . . .'

'No, they're not strong enough.'

I sat down on the bed. I felt embarrassed to just sit and watch her like an idiot without knowing how to help her.

I felt the same way about Grandma Laura.

A tumour had been eating her stomach for two years and she had had loads of operations and each time we had to go and visit her. She lay there, in that little hospital room with the fake leather armchairs, the *People* and *l'Espresso* magazines that only we read, the laminate on the furniture, the pale green walls, the dry croissants in the cafeteria, the grumpy nurses and their hideous white clogs, the disgusting tiles on the plantless little terrace.

And her in that metal bed, pumped with medicines, her mouth open without her false teeth, and my parents watching her in silence, smiling with tight lips while they secretly hoped that she would die as quickly as possible.

I didn't get why we had to go and visit her. Grandma barely understood who we were.

'We're keeping her company. You'd like that too', my mum would say to me.

No, it's not true. It's embarrassing getting visits when you're not well. And when you're dying I bet you want to be left alone. I really didn't get this thing about paying visits.

I looked at my sister. She was trembling all over.

Then, suddenly, I remembered.

What an idiot. I knew exactly where I could find the medicine.

'I'll take care of everything. You stay here, I'll be back soon.'

113

8

Beneath a light rain, I caught the number 30 bus.

I'd been lucky. When I'd left the building, the Silver Monkey had been taking his afternoon nap.

I sat at the back of the bus with my hoodie pulled down over my face. I was a secret agent on a mission to save my sister and nothing would stop me.

The last time we had gone with Grandma to the hospital, shortly before leaving home, she had whispered in my ear, 'Darling, go and get all the medicine from my bedside cabinet and hide it in my bag. Those bloody doctors never give me enough to ease the pain. Don't let anyone see you though.'

I had managed to get them into her bag without anyone noticing.

I got off a short walk from Villa Ornella.

But when I stood in front of the clinic all my courage disappeared. I had promised Grandma that I would go and visit her on my own, but I'd never gone. I just wasn't able to talk to her like we were still at her house. Those times I'd gone with Mum and Dad had been torture.

'Come on, Lorenzo, you can do it,' I said to myself, and I looked over at the car park. No sign of my parents' cars. I bounded up the steps to the entrance of the clinic and cut across the hallway. The nun behind the reception looked up from the computer screen but she only glimpsed a shadow disappearing up the stairs. I ran down the long corridor. It took 3,225 steps. I had counted them on the day they had operated on Grandma. I had spent the whole afternoon in hospital with Dad as Grandma had been in theatre for ages.

I went past the nurses' station. They were laughing. I turned right, and a walking dead man came shuffling towards me in his slippers. He was wearing light blue pyjamas with dark blue hems. White curls poked out of the V-neck of his cardigan. A fresh scar cut across his cheekbone and ended near his mouth. A woman lying on a stretcher was looking at a framed picture of a stormy sea hanging on the wall above her. A little girl came out of a doorway but was immediately pulled back in by her mother's hand.

Room 103.

I waited for my heart to slow and then I turned the door handle.

The urine drainage bag was almost full. Her dentures were soaking in a glass on the bedside table. The drip hung from the IV trolley. Grandma Laura was sleeping in the bed with the bars. Her lips had fallen into her gaping mouth. She was so small and shrunken I could probably have picked her up and taken her away with me.

I moved closer and studied her, biting the inside of my cheek.

She was so old. A pile of bones covered by a scaly wrinkled skin. One leg stuck out from underneath the sheet. She was black and blue and as thin as a rake; her foot was crooked and her big toe was folded inwards like the bone was made of metal wire. She smelled of powder and antiseptic. Her hair, which she always kept held back neatly in a hairnet when she was well, was loose and lay across the pillow, white and long, like a witch's.

She could have been dead. But her face didn't show the peacefulness of a corpse, it bore a stiff expression of sufferance, like her flesh was shot through with a current of pain.

117

I went over to the foot of the bed and covered her leg with the sheet. The suede toiletry bag was in the wardrobe. I opened it and took out all the bottles and boxes of medicine and stuffed them in my pockets. As I was zipping it back up I heard a whisper behind me, 'Lo-re-nzo . . . Is that you?'

I whirled around. 'Yes, Grandma. It's me.'

'Lorenzo, did you come to visit me?' A spasm made her face tighten. She kept her eyes half closed. The clouded eyeballs were surrounded by wrinkled folds.

'Yes.'

'Good boy. Sit down next to me . . .'

I sat next to the bed on a metal stool.

'Grandma, I should be . . .'

'Give me your hand.'

I squeezed her hand. It was warm.

'What time is it?'

I looked at the clock on the wall. 'It's ten past two.'

'In the morning . . .' She moved and squeezed my hand softly. 'Or . . .?'

'In the afternoon, Grandma.'

I had to get out of there. It was too dangerous.

If the nurses saw me they would definitely tell my parents.

Grandma didn't speak, just breathed through her nose like she'd fallen asleep, then she rolled over in search of a more comfortable position.

'Are you in pain?'

She touched her stomach. 'Here . . . It never stops. I'm sorry you have to see me suffer. It's so unpleasant dying like this.' She was pulling her words out one by one, like she was looking for them in an empty box.

'No, don't die,' I murmured, with my eyes fixed on her yellow drainage bag.

She smiled. 'No, not yet. This body of mine does not want to leave yet. It hasn't quite understood that it's all over.'

I wanted to tell her that I had to run, but I didn't have the courage. I stared at the garments hanging from the wooden clothes horse: the blue skirt, the white blouse, the dark red cardigan.

She'll never wear them again, I thought. In fact, they'll put them on her when they lock her in the coffin.

I looked at the opaque glass lampshade hanging from a brass rod on the ceiling. Why was the room so ugly? When someone dies they should have a beautiful room. I would die in my bedroom.

'Grandma, I have to go . . .' I wanted to hug her. Maybe it would be the last time I could. I asked her, 'Can I hug you?'

Grandma opened her eyes and nodded slightly.

I squeezed her gently, squashing my face into her pillow and smelling the pungent odour of medicine, the soap on the pillowcase and the sour smell from her skin.

'I should . . . I have to go and study.' I pulled myself upright.

She took my wrist and sighed. 'Tell me a story . . . Lorenzo. So I won't think about it.'

'Which story, Grandma?'

'I don't know. Whichever you want. A nice story.'

'Right now?' Olivia was waiting for me.

'If you feel like it. It doesn't matter . . .'

'Does it have to be real or imaginary?'

'Imaginary. Carry me off to another place.'

Actually, I did have a story to tell. I had made it up one morning at school. I kept my stories to myself, because if I told them they wilted like cut wild flowers and I didn't like them any more.

But this time was different.

I got more comfortable on the stool. 'So here's the story . . . Grandma, do you remember the little robot you have in your pool in Orvieto? The yellow and purple one you use for cleaning the pool? That little robot has a sort of electronic brain inside him, which learns about the bottom of the pool, so that it can clean it properly, without having to go back over the same spots. Do you remember it, Grandma?' I couldn't work out if she was sleeping or if she was awake.

'This is the story of a little pool-cleaning robot. Its name is K19, like the Russian submarines. So . . . One day, in America, all the generals and the President of the United States meet to decide how to kill Saddam Hussein. They've tried everything they can think of to get rid of him. His house is a fortress in the desert, he's got ground-to-air missiles which are launched as soon as the American rockets come near, and he makes them explode in mid-air. The President of America is in despair — if he doesn't kill Saddam right away, they'll sack him. If his generals don't find a way to get rid of the dictator within ten minutes, he'll send them all to Alaska. Then one general stands up, a little one, who's an expert in computers, and he says he's got an idea. They all shake their heads, but the President tells him to speak up. Shortie begins explaining that Saddam doesn't buy anything at all because he's afraid that bombs will be hidden inside. Once he ordered a pineapple and inside it there was a bomb, which killed his cook. So everything he has inside his house he has had built in his underground laboratories. Televisions, videorecorders, fridges, computers – everything. There is just one thing he is forced to buy elsewhere. His pool-cleaning robots. Saddam's swimming pool is so big that his little robot can't find its way around, while the winds from the desert blow continuously, filling the pool with sand. The best ones, the ones that can clean a pool as huge as his, are made exclusively in America.'

I stopped talking. 'Do you get it, Grandma?'

She didn't answer. Slowly I tried to slip my hand out of hers.

'Go on . . .' she murmured.

'Saddam would go for a swim with his twelve wives and always found the bottom of the pool dirty. So, in the end, even though it's dangerous, he decides to order one from America. He gets one of his aides to buy it, so nobody suspects it's for him. Except that the CIA has intercepted the phone call. The factory has to send it to him next week. General Shortie says he's had a brilliant idea. He'll take the little robot and modify it. He'll put in a super-intelligent computer, which he has just invented, and he'll programme it to kill Saddam. He'll put mini nuclear torpedoes inside the robot, and some batteries that produce two thousand volts of electricity and which can also shoot poison darts.

'The President of the United States is happy. It's a wonderful idea. He tells Shortie to get straight to work. Shortie goes to the little robot factory, he gets one and he works on it for the whole night. He puts a computer inside and he programmes it to kill Saddam, and, just to be sure, anyone else who's swimming with him in the pool. When he has finished he's exhausted, but the little robot is perfect, it looks just like any of the others. Its code name is K19. Except that the next morning the guy who has to send it off comes into work and makes a mistake. He believes that it's one that's been repaired for a family that live near Los Angeles. He packs it up and sends it off. When it

123

gets there the family takes it and puts it in the pool. K19 begins cleaning the bottom – it knows how to do that really well too. But when the dad and the kids get in for a swim they are all killed instantly by an electrical charge that fries them all.'

'Who were they? Finotti's grandkids?' Grandma had lifted her head up off the pillow.

'Who are the Finottis?' I said.

'Marino Finotti, the engineer from Terni . . . Didn't they die in their swimming pool?'

'Nooo, these are Americans, it's got nothing to do with Terni.'

'Are you sure?' She was getting worked up.

'Yes, Grandma, don't worry.' I began telling the story again. 'So . . . the little robot waits for two days, the corpses floating, but Saddam doesn't show up, so, since it's intelligent, it works out that they must have put him in the wrong pool. It uses its caterpillar tracks to climb up the sides and goes off in search of a new pool. The place where they sent it, in America, Grandma, is full of swimming pools – there's one for every house, heaps of them, millions, and so he starts going from one to another, killing anyone who goes for a swim, in search of Saddam. Whenever it runs into another little robot he disintegrates it and then he cleans the pool. It's a massacre. Half of California is wiped out. The army comes in. All the soldiers attack it, shooting it with lasers, but there's nothing they can do. In the end they call for air strikes and start dropping bombs on California. K19 is hit. One of its caterpillar tracks gets broken and he starts swerving all over the place, but he doesn't give up. He goes outside and starts driving down the highway followed by armed tanks that shoot at it. K19 is a wreck. His engine is making a strange noise and he has used all his weapons. He comes to the end of the road and is facing the biggest pool he's ever seen, with very dirty water and waves too. The army is closing in. K19 looks at the pool; it's so big he can't even see where it ends. The sun is setting into it and there are huge floating mattresses on it. Nobody has explained to him that this is the ocean and they're not floating mattresses but ships. K19 doesn't know what to do. He wonders how he will ever manage to clean this never-ending swimming pool. For the first time he's afraid. He gets to the end of the pier, turns around. The army is right there. He's about to fight, but then he thinks again. He jumps quickly into the ocean, and disappears.'

My mouth was dry. I picked up the bottle of water from the bedside table and poured myself a glass.

Grandma didn't move. She'd fallen asleep.

She'd hated the story.

I got up, but Grandma whispered, 'Then what?'

'What do you mean, then what?'

'How does it end?'

That was the end. It felt like a good ending to me.

And, anyway, I hated endings. In endings things always have to be, for better or for worse, fixed up. I liked telling stories of fights for no reason between aliens and earthlings, of space journeys in search of nothing. And I liked wild animals that lived for no reason, that didn't know they were dying. After I saw a film, it drove me crazy the way Dad and Mum always talked about the ending, like the whole story was in the ending and nothing else mattered.

And so, in real life, is the ending the only

important part? Grandma Laura's life was worth nothing and only her death in that ugly clinic mattered? Yes, maybe the story about K19 was missing something, but I liked the way it committed suicide in the ocean. I was about to tell her that that was the ending when, just like that, I thought up another ending.

'This is the ending. Two years later some scientists are on a beach on a tropical island, at night, in the light of the full moon. They're hiding behind a dune with their binoculars and watching the shore. Suddenly the sea turtles come out of the water, they're going to lay their eggs. The turtles climb over the sand, they dig a hole with their legs and they lay their eggs. And K19 comes out too. He's all covered in seaweed and mussels. He climbs slowly up the beach and uses his cater-pillar tracks to dig a deep hole, covers it over and then goes back into the sea with the turtles. The next night a whole heap of little turtles pop out of the sand. And from one of the holes lots of teeny-weeny K19s pop up, like little play tank engines, and they head towards the shore along with all the little turtles.' I took a deep breath. 'That's the end. Did you like it?'

127

Grandma, her eyes closed, nodded and right then the door was flung open and a nurse that looked exactly like John Lennon walked in, carrying a tray of medicine.

We stared at each other for a second, I mumbled a hello and then I ran.

9

The Silver Monkey was wandering aimlessly around the courtyard.

I was studying him from the other side of the street, hidden behind a rubbish bin. Every now and then he'd swish his broom and then he'd stop, like they'd turned off his electricity.

Like an idiot, I hadn't taken my mobile with me and so I couldn't trick him like I did last time. I had spent too much time with Grandma. It was another two hours before he went off duty, and Olivia was expecting me.

After a quarter of an hour Mr Caccia, the engineer from the fourth floor, came home. Then Nihal and the Dachshunds came out of the main door and he started chatting near the fountain with the Silver Monkey. The two of them didn't really get along, but the Silver Monkey had a relative who worked for a travel agency and was able to get him airline tickets at discount prices.

As I stood hidden behind the bin, my legs

started to ache. I cursed myself for having forgotten the phone.

And to top it off, Giovanni the postman turned up too. Nihal's chum. All three of them starting chatting and there was no end in sight. The poor little Dachshunds stared at them forlornly, bursting to go for a piss.

That was it. I had to do something. If they caught me, too bad.

I moved further away and crossed the street. Then I ran up to the wall of our building. It was high, but an old bougainvillea extended unevenly up to its top.

'C'mon, Roma then . . . What else can we do?' I heard the Silver Monkey saying.

'This time they'll pay. Totti's back. Anyway, see you . . .' Giovanni said.

Oh God, he was coming out. I grabbed a branch and a thorn pierced my hand. I braced myself, pulled myself up the wall and with a clumsy leap landed in Mrs Barattieri's garden. Praying nobody would see me I crouched against the wall.

The window that opened into the Silver Monkey's basement was ajar.

At least this was going my way.

I opened it and holding onto the frame I slid down into the half-light. I stretched out my legs looking for somewhere to land and an extreme heat engulfed my left foot. Holding in a scream I tumbled onto the gas cooker and from there, landed on my arse on the floor. I had sunk my shoe into a saucepan of pasta and lentils, which luckily had been turned off and was cooling down.

I stood up, rubbing one of my buttocks.

The lentils were scattered all over the place, like a bomb had exploded.

And now what? If I didn't clean everything up the Silver Monkey would see the mess and think that . . .

I smiled.

Of course, he would think that the gypsies had come into his house again.

I looked around. I had to steal something.

My gaze fell on a statue of Padre Pio which looked like a torpedo. It was covered in a sparkling powder that changed colour depending on the weather.

I picked it up and was about to leave, but then I went back and threw open the fridge.

131

Fruit, a bowl of boiled rice and a six-pack of beer.

I took the beers. When I came out of the doorman's booth the Silver Monkey was still in the courtyard, talking to Nihal.

Limping, and carrying one of my shoes, I went down the stairs which led to the cellars. I turned the key in the lock and flung the door open. 'Look . . . I've got be—'

The statue of Padre Pio slipped out of my hands and shattered on the floor.

Olivia was lying on my bed with her legs open. One arm thrown over the pillow. A dribble of saliva hung off her chin.

I put my hand over my mouth. *She's dead.*

All the wardrobes had been thrown wide open, all the drawers pulled out, all the clothes thrown about, boxes had been gutted. Beneath the bed were open bottles of medicine.

I dragged myself over to the settee without taking my eyes from my sister.

I touched my temples – they were pulsating, a humming in my ears numbed my mind and my eyes hurt.

I was so tired, never in my life had I felt this

tired, every fibre in my body was tired and begged me to rest, to close my eyes.

Yes, it was best that I sleep a bit, just five minutes.

I took my other shoe off and lay down on the settee. I stayed like that, I don't know how long for, staring at my sister and yawning.

She was a dark stain stretched out on a light blue bed. I thought about her blood, not moving in her veins. About red blood turning black, as hard as a scab, and then turning into dust.

Olivia's fingers jerked, like dogs when they dream.

I tried to focus, but my eyes were stinging.

I must have been wrong. It was just my imagination.

Then she moved an arm.

I ran to her and began shaking her. I don't remember what I said to her, I just remember that I picked her up off the bed, I squeezed her in my arms and I knew that I had to take her outside and that I was strong enough to hold her in my arms, like she was an injured dog, and walk with her in my arms along via Aldrovandi, via delle Tre Madonne, viale Bruno Buozzi . . .

Olivia began speaking softly.

'You're alive! You're alive!' I stammered.

I couldn't understand what she was saying.

I put a hand behind her neck and I put my ear up close to her month. 'What? What did you say?'

She gurgled, '. . . some sleeping pills . . .'

'How many did you take?'

'Two pills.'

'Are you all right?'

'Yes.' She couldn't hold her head up straight. 'Much better . . . The Countess had a stash of medicine. Good stuff . . . I'm going to sleep a bit more.'

My eyes hazed over with tears. 'Okay.' I smiled at her. 'Sleep well. Sweet dreams.'

I laid her gently onto the bed and spread a blanket over her.

10

For two days my sister slept, waking up only to pee and to drink. I tidied up the cellar. I killed the mutant and I finished Soul Reaver. I started reading *Salem's Lot* again. I was reading about vampiric metamorphoses, haunted houses and courageous kids capable of facing up to vampires, when my gaze fell upon my sister, who was sleeping wrapped up in a blanket. In my den she was safe, hidden away. Nobody could hurt her.

My mother rang me. 'So, how's it going?'

'Everything's fine.'

'You never call me. If it weren't for me calling you . . . Are you having fun?'

'Loads.'

'Are you sad that tomorrow you have to come back?'

'Yes. A bit . . .'

'What time will you head off?'

'Early. We'll go as soon as we get up.'

'What are you up to today?'

'Skiing. Do you know who I ran into in Tofana?'

'No.'

I looked at my sister. 'Olivia.'

A moment of silence. 'Olivia? Olivia who? Your half-sister?'

'Yes.'

'How about that . . . She came by here a couple of days ago looking for some stuff. Now I get it – maybe she needed some clothes to go skiing. How is she?'

'Good.'

'Really? I wouldn't have expected that. Dad said she's not doing so well . . . Poor thing, she's a girl with a lot of problems. I really hope she finds her way . . .'

'But, Mum, do you care about her?'

'Me?'

'Yes.'

'Yes, I care about her but she's not easy to deal with . . . Are you being good? Are you polite to Alessia's mother? Are you lending a hand? Are you making your bed?'

'Yes.'

'Alessia's mother seems lovely. Say hi to her from me and thank her again.'

'Yes . . . Listen, I have to go now . . .'

'I love you, sweetheart.'

'Me too . . . Oh, Alessia's mother said she'd bring me home when we get back.'

'Wonderful. Give me a call when you get to Rome.'

'Okay. Bye.'

'Bye, darling.'

Olivia was sitting on the settee, her wet hair combed back, and she had on one of the Countess's floral dresses. She rubbed her hands together. 'So how will we celebrate our last night?'

After all that sleep she was a lot better. Her face had softened and she said that her legs and arms didn't hurt as much.

'Dinner together?' I said.

'Dinner together. And what do you suggest?'

'Well . . .' I looked at what we had left in the cupboard. 'We've eaten almost everything. Tuna and artichokes in oil? And wafers for dessert?'

'Perfect.'

I got up and opened the wardrobe. 'I've got a surprise . . .' I showed her the beers.

Olivia's eyes widened. 'You're a star! Where the hell did you find them?'

I smiled. 'In the Silver Monkey's apartment. I stole them from him when I came back from the hospital. They're warm . . .'

'Doesn't matter. You're the best,' she said and with her Swiss Army knife she opened two, and passed one to me.

'I don't like beer . . .'

'Doesn't matter. We have to celebrate.' She put the bottle to her mouth and in one swallow she finished off half. 'God, beer is so good.'

I put the bottle up to my mouth too and pretended that I didn't think it was disgusting.

We set the coffee table with a tablecloth we'd found among the Countess's rags. We lit a candle and polished off the artichokes and two tins of tuna. And biscuits for dessert.

Afterwards, our stomachs full, we flopped onto the settee in the dark of the cellar with our feet up on the coffee table. The flame of the candle lit them up. They were identical. Long and white, with bony toes.

Olivia lit up a Muratti. She puffed out a cloud of smoke. 'Do you remember when we went to Capri one summer?'

The beer had loosened my tongue. 'Not really. I just remember there were loads of steps to climb. And there was a well that lizards came out of. And big lemons.'

'And you don't remember when they threw you into the water?'

I turned to look at her. 'No.'

'We were on Dad's motorboat in front of the Faraglioni.'

'I've seen the motorboat in photos. It was shiny wood. It was called *Sweet Melody II*. There's even a photo where Dad is waterskiing.'

'This sailor, who was all tanned, he had curly hair and a gold chain, used to drive it. You were terrified of the water. As soon as you saw the beach you would scream until they put your armbands on. You wouldn't even get on the ferry if you didn't have them on. Anyway, that day we were out in open water and everyone was swimming and you were wrapped around the ladder like a crab watching us. If anyone suggested you swim you went crazy. Then we caught some sea urchins and we ate them with bread. Dad and the sailor had drunk loads of wine, and the sailor told a story about how to make kids get over their fear of water by throwing them into the sea without water wings or lifejackets. They go under for a bit but afterwards they all learn to swim. You were down in the cockpit playing with your toys, they came up to you from behind, slipped your armbands off and you started wriggling, yelling like they were skinning you alive. I told them to leave you alone, but they wouldn't listen. And that was it, they threw you in the water.'

I listened to her in awe. 'And my mother didn't do anything?'

'She wasn't there that day.'

'And then what happened?'

She smiled. 'You sank. Dad dived in to get you. But after a second you popped up screaming like a shark had bitten you. You began flapping your arms and . . . you swam.'

'Really?'

'Yes, doggy paddle, with your eyes popping out of your head and you grabbed onto the ladder and you jumped out like you'd been dipped in lava.'

'And then what?'

'And then you ran into the cabin and you curled up on the bunk bed trembling and breathing with your mouth open. Dad tried to calm you down, saying that you'd been very good, that you were a great swimmer, that you didn't need the water wings any more. But you kept on crying. You yelled at him to go away.'

'And then what?'

'You fell asleep all of a sudden. You went down like you'd been given an anaesthetic. I've never seen anything like it.'

'And you . . . what did you do?'

'I lay down next to you. Then the motorboat took off. And me and you, we stayed down in the cabin where it smelled of bilge and everything was shaking and rocking.'

'Me and you?'

'Yes.' She took a drag of her cigarette. 'Me and you.'

'How weird. I don't remember anything. Dad never told me about that.'

'Of course he didn't, he fucked up . . . And if

your mother had found out she would've eaten him alive. Can you swim now?'

I shrugged. 'Yes.'

'And you're not afraid of the water?'

'No. I even did swimming for a while. But I gave it up. I can't think with water in my ears. I hate the swimming pool.'

Olivia stubbed out the cigarette in the tuna tin. 'What's the thing you hate most in the world?'

There were so many things. 'Surprise parties, maybe. Two years ago my mother organised one for me. All those people wishing me happy birthday. It was a nightmare. New Year's Eve is another thing I hate. What about you?'

'Me . . . Let me think. I can't stand weddings.'

'Yeah, I hate those too.'

'Hang on!' Olivia got up. 'Look what I found.' She pulled out a square red suitcase. She opened it. There was a record player inside. 'Who knows if it still works.'

We plugged it in and the turntable began spinning. She started looking through a box full of records. 'I can't believe it . . . Look at this, this is fantastic.' She pulled out an LP and showed it to me. 'I love this song.' She placed it on the turntable and together with Marcella Bella she began to sing in a shaky voice: '*Mi ricordo montagne verdi e le corse di una bambina con l'amico mio più sincero, un coniglio dal muso nero . . .*' 'I remember the green mountains and a little girl racing against her dearest friend, a rabbit with a black nose . . .'

I turned down the volume. 'Quiet . . . Quiet . . . They can hear us. Mrs Barattieri, the Monkey . . .'

But Olivia wasn't listening to me. She was dancing in front of me, swaying and singing softly: '*Poi un giorno mi prese il treno, l'erba, il prato e quello che era mio scomparivano . . .*' 'Then one day he took away my train, the grass, the field and what was mine disappeared . . .'

She grabbed my hands and, looking at me with those magnetic eyes of hers, she pulled me towards her. '*Il mio destino è di stare accanto a te, con te vicino più paura non avrò, e un po' bambina tornerò.*' 'My destiny is to be next to you, with you near me I won't be afraid, and I will be a little girl again.'

I sighed and, awkwardly, I began to dance. That's what I hated most. Dancing.

But that evening I danced, and when I danced

I felt something I'd never felt before. I felt alive – it took my breath away. In a few hours I would leave that cellar. And everything might go back to the way it was. And yet I knew that beyond that door the world was waiting for me, and that I would be able to talk to the others like I was one of them. Decide to do things and then actually do them. I could leave. I could go to boarding school. I could change the furniture in my bedroom.

The cellar was dark. I could hear the steady breathing of my sister lying on the settee.

She had finished off five bottles of beer and a packet of Muratti cigarettes.

I wasn't able to fall asleep. I wanted to keep on talking. I was thinking back to the raid on the Silver Monkey, back to when I saw the others leaving for ski week, to the dinner with the beers, my sister and me chatting like adults, dancing to 'Montagne Verdi'.

'Olivia?' I whispered.

She took a while to answer. 'Yes.'

'Are you asleep?'

'No.'

'What will you do when we get out of here?'

'I don't know . . . I might go away.'

'Where to?'

'I have a sort of boyfriend who lives in Bali.'

'Bali? In Indonesia?'

'Yes, he teaches yoga and does massages in a place by the sea full of palm trees. There are loads of colourful fish. I want to work out whether we're still together. I want to try and be his woman for real. If he wants me . . .'

'His woman,' I murmured with my mouth on the pillow.

He was lucky that guy. He could say, 'Olivia is my woman.' I would have liked to go to Bali too. Catch the plane with Olivia. And laugh in the check-in queue without needing to talk. Her and me, flying towards the colourful fish. And Olivia would say to her boyfriend, 'This is Lorenzo, my brother.'

'What's your boyfriend's name?' I asked, struggling to speak.

'Roman.'

'Is he a nice guy?'

'I'm sure you'd like him.'

It was cool that Olivia knew me well enough to know that I'd like her boyfriend. 'Listen, I have to tell you something . . . I said I was going skiing in Cortina because I made a huge mess of things. I was at school and I heard that some of my classmates were going skiing. They hadn't invited me to go. And I really don't care about going away on trips with other people, but when I got home I told Mum that I'd been invited along too. And she believed me and she was happy and she started crying, and I didn't have the guts to tell her the truth so I hid out down here. You know what? Since that day I've been trying to work out why I told her that lie.'

'And have you worked it out?'

'Yes. Because I did want to go. Because I wanted to ski with them – I'm a good skier. Because I wanted to show them the secret slopes. And because I don't have any friends . . . And I wanted to be one of them.'

I heard her getting up.

'Move over.'

I made some room and she lay down next to me and hugged me tightly. I could feel her bony knee. I put one hand on her hip, I could count her rib bones, then I rubbed her back. Underneath my fingers, her pointy vertebrae.

'Olivia, will you promise me something?'

'What?'

'That you won't take drugs ever again. Never ever again.'

'I swear to God. Never again. I won't let that happen to me ever again,' she whispered in my ear. 'And numb nuts, will you promise that we'll see each other again?'

'I promise.'

When I woke up my sister had gone.

She'd left me a note.

Cividale del Friuli

12 June 2010

I have another sip of coffee and read the note again.

Dear Lorenzo,
I remembered that another thing I hate are goodbyes and so I've decided to slip out before you wake up.
Thanks for helping me. I'm happy I found a brother hidden in a cellar.
   Remember to keep the promise.
   Yours,
   Oli
   P.S. Watch out for the Silver Monkey.

Today, after ten years, I will see her again for the first time since that night.

I fold the note up and put it back in my wallet. I pick up my suitcase and walk out of the hotel.

A cold wind is blowing, but a pale sun has made room in between the clouds and is warming my forehead. I turn up the collar of my coat and cross the street. The suitcase wheels rattle on the cobbles.

This is the street. I walk in through a stone entrance that opens into a square courtyard full of cars.

A doorman points me in the right direction. I open the glass door.

'Can I help you?'

'My name's Lorenzo Cuni.'

He gestures for me to follow as he walks down a corridor. He stops in front of a door. 'Here we are.'

'My suitcase?'

'It's best you leave it here.'

The room is big, covered in white tiles. It's cold.

My sister is lying on a table. A sheet covers her up to her neck.

I move closer. I struggle to put one foot in front of the other.

'Is it her? Do you recognise her?'

'Yes . . . it's her.' I move a little closer. 'How did you manage to find me?'

'Your sister's purse had a little piece of paper with your number on it.'

'Can I stay with her?'

'Five minutes.' He goes out and closes the door.

I lift up the sheet and take her yellow hand. She is skinny like when we were in the cellar. Her face is relaxed and she is as beautiful as ever. She looks like she's sleeping.

I bend over and put my nose up against her neck.

Olivia Cuni was born in Milan on 25 September 1976 and died at the Bar della stazione in Cividale del Friuli on 9 January 2010 of an overdose. She was thirty-three years old.

Me and You

Niccolò Ammaniti

ABOUT THIS GUIDE

We hope that these discussion questions will
enhance your reading group's exploration of
Niccolò Ammaniti's *Me and You*. They are meant
to stimulate discussion, offer new viewpoints and
enrich your enjoyment of the book.

More reading group guides and additional
information, including summaries, author tours
and author sites for other fine Black Cat titles
may be found on our Web site,
www.groveatlantic.com.

QUESTIONS FOR DISCUSSION

1. Angst-ridden teen Lorenzo Cuni takes center stage in this brief novel as it charts one momentous week in his young life. Begin your discussion of the work by considering how well you got to know him in this short period of time. How appealing a character is he to you? Does your opinion change as the narrative unfurls?

2. While Lorenzo's self-induced confinement in the family cellar begins with his need to pretend that he is away on a ski vacation with his friends, it grows to become more than that. Talk about the evolution of "Operation Bunker" and what it means to Lorenzo. Does he look forward to his time there? Do you think he has expectations for the week or does he ultimately view it as a means to an end?

3. Consider how the author manages to speak volumes in such a slim text. Look at his language choices to understand how he can say so much in so few words. Talk about the cinematic quality of the text. Did you find the narrative enigmatic at all due to its brevity?

4. How far would you agree that one of the novel's central themes is authenticity of self? How does this manifest itself in Lorenzo's life? Consider his constant attempts to hide his true nature to fit in with the people around him. Why is it so debilitating for him? Discuss instances in the novel where other characters hide from themselves or hide themselves from each other.

5. Continue your discussion of this theme and look at the underground cellar in the light of this statement: "On my own I was happy, with the others I always had to pretend" (p. 38). By hiding in the cellar, Lorenzo dupes his parents into thinking that he has achieved normalcy, that he has conformed to everyone else's expectations. Ironically, what does his time in the cellar allow him to do?

6. Discuss Lorenzo's relationship with his mother. Do you think that the author presents her as a stereotype, or at least as a universal modern mother? Do you sense underlying criticism in the depiction of Ms. Cuni? How much, if at all, does Lorenzo's attitude toward his mother's concerned parenting change during his time underground away from her?

7. In a striking scene Lorenzo witnesses his mother through the eyes of outsiders as they verbally abuse her for her role in a car accident. His response is to faint. What did you take away from this? What do you think the scene said about Lorenzo and his mother?

8. How fair is it to say that Lorenzo's parents main hope is for their son to be viewed as normal and socially acceptable? Why is this so important to them?

9. With cunning perceptiveness and blatant manipulation Lorenzo knows very well how to play his parents against each other. He tells his mother, "Dad said I have to be independent. That I have to have my own life. That I have to break away from you." Do you think he has any idea of the truth behind this? Find other examples of his manipulation.

10. Discuss the sense of the absurd throughout the novel, whether it is, for example, the premise of Lorenzo hiding from his parents in their own basement or the scene in which he steals pain medication from his dying grandmother. Find other examples and figure out how the author mines these scenes for their poignant details and creates highly realistic scenarios.

11. "Lorenzo, you're like a cactus: you grow without bothering anyone, you just need a drop of water and a bit of light" (p. 27). How prescient was the old nanny from Caserta in saying this to Lorenzo? How far would you agree that other people were the problem for young Lorenzo?

12. Consider Lorenzo's childhood as a whole and find instances where he understands that he needs to fit into society, especially the primal society of the school yard. Talk about the difference between knowing the importance of fitting in and wanting to fit in. How do these differences affect Lorenzo? When do the two ideas meld together and become one and the same for him?

13. Why does Lorenzo choose the history high school instead of the mathematics one. What does this say about him? About his father?

14. The novel opens with a description of the scientific theory of Batesian mimicry in which "a harmless animal species takes advantage of its similarity to a toxic or poisonous species . . . imitating its coloring and behavior." This classic means of survival among animals is used by Lorenzo with

great effectiveness as he adopts the mantra "Imitate the dangerous ones" (p. 37). How is he able to continue this charade with his parents? Does he convince himself? What is his biggest fear during this time of his life?

15. One of the most developed and sympathetic characters in the book is the canasta-playing, Bloody Mary–drinking grandmother. Why do you think Lorenzo likes her so much? What does she represent in the novel?

16. While Lorenzo struggles to survive at school he is struck by Alessia Roncato and her tightly knit group of friends. What does he find so alluring about them—about Alessia especially? Why is this?

17. Lorenzo's life away from the confines of society is interrupted suddenly by the arrival of Olivia, his half-sister from his father's previous marriage. Discuss the reasons that Lorenzo is so angry to see her, and reluctant to help her.

18. Consider the way that Lorenzo shows true allegiance to his father when Olivia speaks ill of him, and discuss whether perhaps he grows to learn that

the image he has of his father may not be the only one. People are not always as they appear. Does this apply to other people in the novel? His mother?

19. "Something inside me snapped. The giant that had been holding me up against his stone chest had let me go" (p. 110). Talk about this passage and what it means in the narrative as a whole. Why do you think Lorenzo decides to help his sister now, knowing that she is a junkie? To what extent would you say that this is the defining moment in the novel? Why, or why not? How has Lorenzo changed?

20. Talk about the sense of life and hope that springs up in the presence of Olivia and Lorenzo as they begin to appreciate each other as siblings, and as damaged individuals. What can they offer each other, and what do they learn from each other? What do you think Olivia's feelings are for Lorenzo given the hellish life she is living?

21. Would you consider Olivia as an authentic person? She is certainly not trying to please her father but is she hiding from her true self in other ways? What do you think it is about her that inspires Lorenzo so greatly?

22. Olivia and Lorenzo exchange hopeful promises as their week together draws to an end. As a reader is it possible to believe that their dreams will exist in the world beyond the cellar or do you sense that the real world will extinguish them? How far are the promises a young boy's naïve wishes taken up by a young woman looking for salvation?

23. Lorenzo undergoes some deep transformations down in the cellar. How hard do you think it is for him to be honest with himself and comprehend the reason for his lie to his mother? Do you think he has rediscovered who he is, or instead has become a different version of himself, an authentic one? Why do you think it is such a revelation to him that he wants to have friends, and have fun? How much of this understanding came from Olivia? How do you think he will survive in the real world outside?

24. Why do you think the author chose to sandwich Lorenzo's coming of age between the bookends of the Cividale del Friuli chapters from ten years later? What effect do these chapters have on the rest of the novel? Do they change the tone, the central message?

25. When Lorenzo tells a story to his dying grandmother he thinks about the human need for closure. How far would you agree with him that humans crave this sense of ending? In the light of his thoughts discuss the ending of the novel. Would you have preferred an open ending with Lorenzo ready to embrace the world and his sister promising never to touch drugs again? Or were you pleased with the closure of the ending?

26. Ultimately, would you view the novel as tragic? Or as hopeful? Why?